THE EXPLODED SOUL

JEFFREY THOMAS

Interior and cover design by Cyrus Wraith Walker

Editor and Publisher, Joe Morey

ISBN: 978-1-957121-73-4

DARK MOONS

Dark Moons is an Imprint of
Weird House Press
Central Point, OR 97502
www.weirdhousepress.com

CONTENTS

PART ONE:

Sinan

A person of Earth with some knowledge of history might have described Honh Yungen as a highwayman, or likened him to the robber/murderer bands called "thugs" in ancient India. Honh Yungen himself, though, had no awareness of the planet Earth, nor did the planet Earth have any awareness of Yungen's planet—Sinan—because those two worlds resided in separate planes of existence from each other.

Honh had built his own house, a cabin raised up from the jungle floor on wooden legs, and he lived in it alone. Most times. That is, when he didn't keep a captive around for a few days, to entertain himself.

The wood of the cabin ranged in color from white to purple to black, depending on the type of tree he had taken it from. Out of a sense of artistry, however, he hadn't mixed these colors randomly. The sturdy legs upon which the cabin rested, to keep out large animals, were all white, whereas the log walls of the cabin were all of purple wood. The door and window shutters were made of long, straight branches of black wood, tightly bound together with cord. The roof was thatch, and thus it was blue—and that was because all the foliage on the planet Sinan, from the slimmest blade of grass to the largest tree frond, was in some shade of blue, be it pale pastel or deepest indigo or anything in-between. Most vegetation, though, tended toward a vivid sapphire color. Honh didn't know why this was, because he couldn't imagine trees and plants that were anything but blue.

In fact, Honh's skin itself was a shade of blue—as was the case for all Sinanese. Again, he couldn't imagine it being any other way.

Honh lived within a day's walk from several main paths through the rainforest, connecting one village to another. He had chosen this spot for his base of operations well, because it was only a two days' walk to the great city of Haikan, besides. These narrow, unpaved roads were close enough to home for him to lie in wait for prey, but not so close that anyone investigating a disappearance would immediately come knocking at his cabin door. Not that it hadn't happened, twice before. Both times Honh—smiling politely, offering the stern-faced policemen tea—had explained that he was a hunter, and had shown off his traps and the fur pelts and beautiful lizard skins hanging from racks to dry. And it wasn't a lie; he *was* a hunter, wasn't he? But he certainly didn't keep the hides of the people he ambushed and dispatched. He took their money, their clothing, and any food they might be carting, and he had even slaughtered draught animals such as yubos a few times for meat. He either used these goods for himself, or—if his victims had jewelry or other such valuables—he was careful to sell them only in Haikan, where street vendors were common, not in any small village.

He had suggested to the investigating policemen, those two times, that the missing travelers had probably been set upon by snipes, because those creatures were plentiful in that area. Again, there was some truth to this. For one, he himself had been stalked by a lone snipe on numerous occasions, and had even had to shoot and kill several with his rifle over the years, and once he had been chased up into his cabin by a pack of them. On that occasion, he'd counted himself lucky to have reached safety and barred his door in time. Usually, though, snipes were content to scavenge...and this they did on the bodies of his victims, which he left in the forest for them. So, it wasn't really lying that the snipes had got to these people, after all...and the teeth marks found on their bones, if the bones were ever recovered, only added a semblance of truth to his story.

When not lying in wait for travelers on any of these remote paths, Honh did indeed lay traps for small game, and hunt midsized creatures with his rifle. At this very moment, he crouched by one of his traps, a simple snare made from twisted wire placed in front of a burrow, but he found it empty. Perhaps the animal had abandoned this den, but another might just as readily be caught venturing into it to take it over. He'd check back on his next rounds.

Just as Honh was preparing to rise and move on to his next trap—this one a more involved "twitch-up snare," that would catch an animal around the neck, then release a bent sapling to fling the animal into the air and break its neck—he realized he was being watched.

He turned his head slowly, so as not to spook whatever it was that spied on him, and closed his fist tighter on the handle of the machete he carried. When he met the eyes that peered out at him through a mosaic of leaves and their shadows, he was both grateful and alarmed. Grateful that he had sensed the creature's gaze before it could sneak up and take him by surprise, and alarmed that the creature was a snipe.

Honh rose slowly, hoping the animal would be cowed when it saw him grow taller. Snipes were smart; perhaps smart enough that a machete was a thing to be feared, so Honh turned its blade back and forth to catch flashes of the light that came in broken shafts through the jungle canopy.

"There, there," Honh murmured in his native language, the only language he knew. "You don't want to do anything stupid, now, do you?"

He counted on the fact that, alone, snipes were not typically bold enough to attack a person face-to-face, unless they were wounded and hunting was difficult, or unless the prey was a child or elderly person.

As Honh rose to his full height, however, he saw a second pair of eyes glimmering back there behind a screen of foliage, not far from the first. Then, the barest rustle of undergrowth, and he risked a glance to his right. He couldn't see it, but he knew he had just heard a third. So...a pack, then. That wasn't good, not at all. In packs, snipes were decidedly less wary. And smart as they were—though no one knew exactly how intelligent they might be—this pack might be aware that Honh Yungen was not close enough to his elevated cabin to outrun them to shelter.

"Shit, shit, shit," Honh muttered, wondering if he could unsling his rifle from his back in time to point it at the snipes before they charged.

A subtle rustle of underbrush to his left. He didn't look; didn't need to. He knew what was happening: they were moving to surround him. Even now, there might be one behind him, but at this moment that was the only direction Honh hadn't seen or heard one of them, so that was the direction in which he chose to escape.

As Honh spun around and bolted, the lead snipe came bursting from the vegetation to give pursuit. The others leapt after it.

Honh didn't look back to see how many there were, though he guessed it was just those four...maybe six at most. They didn't tend to travel in large packs. But *just* four was enough snipes to take a man down and tear his throat out.

As he plummeted breathlessly through the forest, praying that his feet didn't become entangled in a vine or root, Honh didn't need to glance back to see what the pursuing creatures looked like; he knew only too well. The canine quadrupeds were a pallid, cadaver-like blue in color, and as skeletal-looking as cadavers besides.

Should he drop his machete, try taking the rifle from his back while on the run? Awkward to pull off without slowing his momentum, and he was afraid that by the time he had the weapon in hand and whirled around to confront the pack, they'd be leaping through the air at him. Honh thought his best bet was probably to jump up into a tree and climb high enough into its branches that he could then arm himself with his rifle and fire down at them. The rest would no doubt flee, and keep away thereafter, if he took out one or two of them. But just then, as he frantically took note of the selection of trees before him, Honh recalled that just a bit further ahead was the opening of an old burial tunnel. He believed he might just make it...

The foremost snipe snapped at his ankle, trying to catch hold of him and trip him up...pull him down...but Honh swiped his machete down behind him without looking. Fortunately, the heavy blade connected with the snipe's skull and not his own calf. The snipe gave no yelp of pain, as snipes never emitted so much as a growl, though he could tell it faltered behind him...perhaps mortally wounded. Had he just bought himself enough time?

There it was, in the side of a mounded slope in the jungle floor: the mostly overgrown mouth of the tomb.

Traditionally, Sinanese dead were slathered in a bright yellow mineral concoction to mummify the body, which was then wrapped in a huge blue leaf as if in a shroud, the finished package inserted into one of the many slots dug into the sides of the burial tunnel...such tunnels existing extensively beneath the jungle floor, like the nests of giant ants. It was a sin of the highest order—said to bring bad luck upon a person and all their descendants—to ever disrespect the dead interred therein by stealing their clothing or any jewelry they might wear. Even still, most families refrained from dressing their dead in anything of real value, just in case...but Honh Yungen was more hungry than he was superstitious, not to mention he had no children and hence no descendants to be concerned about. If he was to be damned to some punitive afterlife, he had bought his ticket many times over, and so he had already stripped whatever he could from every body in this particular tunnel years ago. Anyway, the dead here were those from an obscure village that had long ago vanished. Either it had broken up or moved on, or the corpses in this tunnel constituted the last of them.

Honh plunged through the leaves that overgrew the opening, stumbled on its lower edge but luckily didn't go down onto hands and knees. Here, in this narrow throat of hardpacked dirt, he could not very well be surrounded. Beyond, in the darkness of the burial chamber proper, the robbed dead awaited him, and their spirits might bc watching him just now and hoping that this was the day Honh Yungen would be punished for his sins against them. Well, let them crave his destruction all they wanted, because Honh felt this tunnel had actually proved his salvation. Once inside, he whirled to face the opening, hoping the snipes might not at first understand where their prey had disappeared to. At last, he unslung his long hunting rifle, slender and black and loaded with a clip of five copper-jacketed expanding bullets. This rifle was his one great indulgence and his pride and joy.

He heard them out there, snuffling, though he couldn't see them yet through the obscuring blue leaves, made translucent with the sunlight. He considered taking a blind shot, but decided to wait until one of them dared push its snout through the opening. Actually blowing the head off one of them would give the others the surest message.

He waited...and yet instead of coming through the opening, the dog-like creatures gathered out there seemed to be hesitating. Were they even smarter than he'd given them credit for? Knowing that he, the hunted, had turned the tables on them and resumed his rightful role as the hunter? Though they made no vocalizations whatsoever to communicate with each other or convey their feelings, he thought he sensed actual fearfulness.

Then, some dramatic rustling out there suggested to him that the snipes had suddenly turned about and loped back into the forest, to disappear and track more vulnerable prey.

Could it be a trick? Were they *that* smart...to trick him into letting down his guard, into lowering his formidable rifle and emerging from the burial tunnel like unwary game, only to put its head through a waiting snare?

As Honh wondered about this, he became aware of a dim bluish glow around him...not enough to illuminate the throat of the tunnel, let alone reveal the honeycombs bearing dozens of mummies in the chamber behind him, but noticeable nonetheless. It reminded him of the faint bioluminescence the snipes themselves gave off in the dark. Was someone behind him, shining a lantern or such at him? But when Honh turned to look, he saw only the darkness beyond where the dead would be filed, where the tomb widened out somewhat.

Then, finally realizing the source of the glow, Honh looked down at his own body. It was *he*, somehow, who suddenly appeared to be giving off a soft bioluminescence. And yet, this radiance also included his clothing...the rifle in his hands...

"What is this?" he cried out, shocked and afraid, as the luminosity became more pronounced. Now his body's glow clearly lit the tunnel's earthen walls. "Am I cursed?" he shrieked. "You bastards...is this your revenge on me?"

A strange feeling came over him...a sensation or multiple sensations he couldn't even separate from each other, let alone put into words. As if his very body might come apart all at once, separating into every individual particle it was composed of, only for these particles to fly off into all directions...each of them in search of some *other* body to become a part of.

And then, the glow flared blindingly...and went out. Once again, the throat of the tomb was dark. And just as the strange light had vanished, so too had Honh Yungen vanished. Once again, only the dead occupied that burial tunnel beneath the rainforest's floor.

After a while, the pack of snipes became curious and stole closer to the tunnel mouth again. They listened, and the alpha finally gathered the courage to push its snout through the overgrown leaves and peer inside.

Even though it saw nothing there—or perhaps *because* it saw nothing there, where the hunter had been—the snipe turned abruptly and fled back into the jungle once again, taking the rest of its pack with it.

PART TWO:

Port Haven

Captain Robert Fuseli sat alone at a table at the back of the mall's food court, a cup of to-go coffee in front of him, gazing out a row of windows at the dwarf planet Pluto. In the interest of safety, of course, the windows were actually large viewscreens, but they accurately revealed what lay beyond this gently-curving wall of Port Haven station.

Port Haven was a massive orbital space station consisting primarily of two rotating rings, from which projected eight docking arms per ring. The arms projecting from the lower ring—though, in space could there really be an upper or lower?—were for the coming and going of civilian ships, transporting personnel and visitors or else delivering cargo. The upper ring's eight docking arms held military ships of various classes; everything from destroyers on down to individual fighter craft. In addition to this, there was a great military complex stationed down on the surface of Pluto itself, not to mention another base on the moon Charon. Charon was actually like a dwarf planet in itself, so large was it in relation to Pluto, the two of them waltzing around each other like lovers on their 248 year-long orbit around the sun.

Meanwhile, Port Haven orbited Pluto, as if it meant to cut in on the dance. Port Haven and the military bases on Pluto and Charon were the outermost line of defense for the solar system in which lay that supposed gem of the galaxy: Earth.

Earth may once have been a gem, Fuseli reflected as he sipped his coffee, but these days he thought he'd rather live even in the high-crime colony called Punktown, on the planet Oasis. Still, though Fuseli hadn't actually been to Earth in months—not since his return from his last mission, and the inquiry regarding said mission—he still felt it hard to break free of its gravity, metaphorically speaking. However blighted, Earth was the place of his birth; of the birth of the human race. Poised out here on Port Haven station seemed the best compromise for him. Here, with the vastness of space stretching infinitely just beyond the doorstep of the solar system, but with Earth still reassuringly within arm's reach. (Or was that, held at arm's length?) Sometimes this felt to Fuseli like a comfortable spot to be in...while other times it felt like limbo. As if he hovered in indecision about which direction to move in. Backward, toward his origins, or outward... outward...never to look back again.

Fuseli regarded Pluto with his eyes—its extensive patch of rusty red in the south contrasting with the dwarf planet's bright, icy white "heart" in a kind of yin and yang—while his mind wandered far beyond. He was in this faraway mode, lulled by the combined echoing voices of other mall-goers congregated in the food court, when he sensed a presence approaching his table. His instincts as a soldier snapped him to alertness instantly. He didn't expect any enemies to come at him here on Port Haven, of all places, but one never knew...especially after the controversy of his last mission.

He saw it was no enemy coming toward him, but rather one of the few people he really trusted in this solar system or any other he'd been to in his travels. Colonial Forces General Aaron Stroud was Port Haven's commander, a responsibility Fuseli wouldn't have wished on any enemy of his he hadn't killed. With his grandfatherly good looks and silvery crewcut, Stroud was almost too perfect a specimen...if you were unaware that beneath his camo pants, two insect-like prosthetic limbs carried him in place of legs. Stroud had lost the originals during the Red War. Fuseli—a military medical officer—had once offered to have new legs cloned for Stroud, that he would then attach himself, but Stroud had snorted and said, "What, are you going to try taking my medals away from me, too?"

Stroud was looking at Fuseli sternly as he approached the table, but he couldn't help smiling once he reached it. Behind the general, two armed guards dressed in gray-patterned camo uniforms, like Stroud, remained standing at a polite distance. You just never could be sure, even here on Port Haven.

Meanwhile, Fuseli wore civilian clothes and a black visored sports cap, as if he'd decided to go undercover today. And he had, really. Fuseli himself was fifty, dark-haired, with sharp features, intense eyes, and a neatly-trimmed mustache and goatee. Taking a seat opposite him, Stroud nodded at the bracelet-like wrist comp Fuseli wore. Its screen was dark.

"You shouldn't be able to turn that thing off, you know, Bob," Stroud said. "What, did you hack it yourself or have someone do it for you?"

"Well, I figured since I'm in civilian mode lately, there'd be no harm in having a little privacy."

"You're never in civilian mode, my friend."

"Yeah? I don't feel too plugged into things lately."

"You feeling sorry for yourself? Well, that's why I'm here...after you forced me to come looking for you on these poor legs of mine."

"Like you walked all the way from your office instead of taking a tram. So why is it you came looking for me? They decided to court martial me, after all?"

"Jesus, will you stop with the self pity, already?" Stroud leaned forward to plant his arms on the table top, but withdrew them when he realized how sticky it was. He tossed a disapproving look at a robot that was wiping down a table nearby. Actually, the robot looked like it could use some wiping down itself. Looking back to Fuseli, Stroud said, "I've got a job for you, Bob."

"Now I think it's *you* who's feeling sorry for me."

"Just shut up and listen. This isn't just some bone I'm throwing you, but something major. Have you heard there was an accident on Titania, or don't you even turn on your wrist comp to check your memos?"

"What happened? Was it that helium-3 base there?" Fuseli was referring to an operation that mined helium-3 from the gas giant Uranus. The mining operation had its headquarters—and stored the mined helium-3, pending distribution—on Titania, which was the largest of Uranus' over two-dozen moons.

"No. There's another base on Titania, Bob; a secret operation. A team of Coleopteroids have been working with us there, to help us develop our own long-range teleportation systems."

"Really? The Bedbugs, huh?"

Stroud grimaced. "Don't call them that, Bob...it's Coleopteroids. Anyway, doing this research on Titania has kept the project out of prying eyes...but mostly, it was in case of an accident such as this, should it have catastrophic effects."

"And did it?"

"Not as bad as it might have been, I guess, in that not all the personnel were killed."

"You sure this wasn't a terrorist attack?" Fuseli asked.

"Looks like a straight mishap with the testing."

"Okay...so you need me to lead a medical team, is it?"

"They have medical personnel stationed there. There weren't many injuries, in that those who were directly in the testing area were all killed...and those who were elsewhere in the facility were not killed. That goes for both humans and Coleopteroids."

Fuseli's brow furrowed. "What is it you need me to do there, then?"

"The teleportation subjects were convicts, some with life sentences. They were going to have their sentences significantly reduced for cooperating, plus given a payout. Four subjects were killed in the blast. Only one survived. He was still in transit, returning from another test site on the planet Jötunn. You know it?"

"Yeah...the planet Port Cygon orbits."

"Right. So, apparently this one test subject was teleporting back from the Jötunn site at the same time the accident occurred."

"Uh-oh. So did he make it back in one piece?"

"Not exactly. I guess you could say he made it back in two pieces."

"But he's still alive?"

"You don't get it, Bob." Stroud leaned across the food court table, stickiness be damned. "Now there's two of him...in a sense. If it was easy to explain, you wouldn't need to go there to help us understand it."

"Two of him...in a sense. You're being cryptic just to entice me, aren't you? Okay, I'll play...but just tell me this much. Generally speaking, in what sense is there two of this test subject now?"

"The original is male. The other one that ported back from Jötunn with him is a female."

PART THREE:

Titania

-1-

The E.C.S. Khopesh was a small military patrol craft carrying twelve individuals, including pilot and copilot. Launched directly from Port Haven—and powered by a q-drive that utilized quantum particles in space for fuel—the Khopesh would arrive at the Titania research base in roughly twenty-three hours, delivering its two highest-ranking passengers: Captain Robert Fuseli and the man he had asked to accompany him, Lieutenant Morris Tarragon.

Even reclining in his seat, Tarragon cut an imposing figure, matched by his usual imposing expression. The Black man's jaw and cheeks were pockmarked with scars, inflicted when he'd once been taken prisoner by the Cepha race and subjected to torture, while his bald head glowed with the passenger cabin's subdued lighting. Fuseli had never trusted a man more, and liked to have Tarragon along with him on an assignment—usually in charge of security—whenever it was possible. Himself long acquainted with Tarragon and equally impressed with him, General Stroud had agreed to let Fuseli have the lieutenant at his side once again. Especially since lately Tarragon, like Fuseli, had been itching for something to do, after the controversial nature of their last mission together.

At the moment, though, Tarragon's eyes were closed, while Fuseli sat reading from his wrist comp—which Stroud had lectured him not to shut down again.

Not that he needed to be told, while on assignment. It was while he sat reading, drifting toward dozing off himself, that Fuseli heard a man speaking to him and looked that way. It was a young Colonial Forces corporal, sitting directly across the aisle from him. Like Fuseli and Tarragon, the corporal wore a camouflage uniform of gray and black patterns, though the two officers wore black greatcoats over theirs, and the black berets of Special Ops.

"Excuse me, sir," the soldier said, grinning. At least he kept his tone hushed, so as not to disturb Tarragon, though Fuseli knew his friend was probably listening in. "I just wanted to tell you how I've followed your career, sir, and how much I admire you! It's an honor to be headed to Titania as part of your security detail."

"Thank you, Corporal..."

"Corporal Alban Hoxha, sir." The young man's face went from grinning to grave. "I just wanted you to know, sir, that myself and every single person I know stood behind you a hundred percent after all hell broke out on planet W-18. I mean, what were you supposed to do, sir? You got the survivors of your team out of there alive and back home in one piece. If you hadn't done what you did, they'd have all been killed...and you and Lieutenant Tarragon, there, too! You wouldn't have had to kill so many of the people on that planet if they hadn't been trying to kill you!"

"Trying to *eat* us," Fuseli said.

"Exactly! Right? Were you supposed to just say—" Corporal Hoxha spread his arms "—here I am, come and get me? And yet, of course, you have all these bleeding hearts who think that's exactly what you should have done. Sacrificed the few for the many, even if the many..."

"Wanted to eat us," Fuseli said.

Another Colonial Forcer leaned around Hoxha to join the conversation. She was a young Black woman, with a great puff of hair gathered at the back of her head. With her huge liquid eyes and the smooth dome of her forehead, Fuseli found her beautiful, though he wondered how she got that hair into a helmet. Oh, to be young again.

"It is sad, though, sir," the young woman said, "that those people were in the state they were in...starving to death like that."

"I'd be the last person to disagree with you, Private..."

"Private Amaka Sunday, sir."

"Pleased to meet you two."

"I've been detailed on Titania before, sir," Hoxha went on, "but I was rotated out after three months. That's why I'm in your team. I've worked with their security chief, Lieutenant Tamati. Let me tell you, he's a tough one...no nonsense, that guy."

"He can't be all that tough," Fuseli said.

"Sir?"

"I mean, if he was really tough, he'd have taught you to be less talkative. And not to talk to your commanding officer like he's your buddy at the strip club."

Hoxha's face dropped and his cheeks flushed, as if he were trying to disguise himself as a whole new person. "Sir...I'm sorry, sir..."

Fuseli smiled. "I'm just teasing you, soldier. Guess I'm bored. It's either tease you for the next twenty-two hours, or maybe try to catch a nap. What do you think I should do?"

Fuseli noticed that Amaka had sunk back into her seat, facing forward nervously herself.

"Um, I think...I think," Hoxha stammered, "you might want to catch some rest before you get to Titania, sir. It sounds like a real serious situation there...I hear."

"That's a great idea, Corporal. Thanks for your advice." Fuseli nestled back into his seat and shut his eyes.

Out of restlessness, and a desire to get away from Corporal Hoxha for a while as he chatted loudly with the more subdued Private Sunday, Fuseli left his seat in the passenger cabin—where most of those aboard the craft were situated—and went up front to the cockpit to sit behind the pilot and copilot. When both pilots acted flustered upon his appearance, as if wondering whether they should jump up from their seats to salute him, Fuseli told them not to let his presence make them nervous. They were military, of course, and of lesser rank, but he was sure they were also intimidated by his reputation.

Fuseli had known they were coming up on Uranus, and thus nearing their destination. Sure enough, there it was outside the front viewport, which was an actual window, and on various screens besides. The main viewscreen enhanced the planet's lovely blue-green color—the result of methane present in an atmosphere primarily composed of hydrogen and helium—and also emphasized its thin rings, the radical slant of which gave away how the planet was tilted in its orbit, almost spinning on its side. They couldn't see it from here, but somewhere down in that ball of icy gas floated a low-orbit space station called Port Urano. This was the largely automated mining operation that extracted helium-3 from the atmosphere. Fuseli knew there were several similar helium-3 harvesting operations in the atmosphere of Jupiter.

There was a beep at the cockpit door, and Private Amaka Sunday identified herself. Fuseli indicated for the copilot to unlock the door for her. Perhaps wanting to escape Corporal Hoxha for a while herself, Amaka entered the cockpit and handed Fuseli a cup of coffee. He arched a brow at her, and she explained, "I noticed you ordered your coffee black, sir."

"I thought you were a soldier, Private...not a stewardess."

He thought he could almost hear her teeth crunching into her tongue as she bit it.

"That was thoughtful of you," he added. "I could use a pick-me-up, since we're almost there and I suspect I'll be diving right into things. Have a seat."

"Thank you, sir." Amaka took the other of the two seats directly behind the pilot and copilot.

Fuseli leaned forward between the pilots and asked, "Are you two going right back to Port Haven, or staying on Titania with us?"

"You've got us for the duration, sir...however long that is," the pilot replied. She was Lieutenant Dalia Halabi, in her thirties and rather petite in build, though Stroud had assured Fuseli she was an experienced fighter pilot with multiple pirate kills to her name, and was hence more than capable of keeping him safe on the way to his destination. The burqa that tightly framed her face was the same camouflage pattern as her uniform.

The copilot was Lieutenant Christopher Rix, who was also in his thirties and usually teamed with Lieutenant Halabi, thus having had his hand in bringing down some space pirates, too. Fuseli liked them both for that reason alone.

Out of curiosity about their fighting exploits, and to put them more at ease about him watching them work, Fuseli chatted with the pilots a bit as they moved on from Uranus toward Titania. Plus, it killed time, not to mention took his mind off the mystery he had to face once they arrived. Rather than speculate too much about the situation, he wanted to go in with a fresh perspective and open mind. Meanwhile, Amaka remained up front with him and simply listened to their conversation.

"Ever been down to Titania yourself, sir?" Halabi asked him, having loosened up by now.

"Never touched down...just passed through the neighborhood. Figured it's much like most of the moons in our system. That is to say, not much of anything. But you've made runs back and forth there multiple times, I take it?"

"Yes sir, shuttling crew from Port Haven...some to the mining headquarters, but mostly to this research station. Of course, Rix and I haven't seen it since they had that explosion there...or whatever it was."

"Guess we'll soon find that out—I hope," Fuseli said. "Though they've already got their regular team looking into that, I take it. My concern is mostly about one of their test subjects. And I hope we'll find out what the deal is with him—or *them*—sooner rather than later."

"I don't know what to think about that situation, sir."

"Nor do I, just yet. Nor do I."

"We're coming up on Titania, now, sir," Lieutenant Rix cut in.

Fuseli got up from his seat, the better to peer at the pilots' arrays of viewscreens and holographic monitors.

"So I see," he said.

-2-

Titania.

The eighth largest moon in the solar system was not even half the radius of Earth's moon, and on the Earth Colonies Ship Khopesh's main screen it looked like a uniformly reddish-gray ball of granite, though it was actually sheathed in a mantle of ice. It hardly seemed deserving of its fanciful name, Titania being the queen of the fairies in Shakespeare's play *A Midsummer Night's Dream*, though another name for the moon was Uranus III. Fuseli felt that undistinguished moniker was more fitting. Though, the part of Fuseli that was an explorer thought it would be quite the adventure to visit the subterranean ocean that lay between Titania's icy mantle and its rocky core. Maybe he'd take a vacation there after this job was done, he joked with himself.

As the Khopesh neared the moon, so that it soon filled most of the front window, the research base could be seen magnified on some of the pilots' various screens. Then, a man's voice came over the cabin speakers. It was singing, and not too well.

"*Calling occupants...of interplanetary craft.*"

Rix leaned toward his mic. "We're here, Research Base Gertrude. Ready for descent."

Leaning on the back of Halabi's seat, Fuseli asked, "What's with that hailing message? Security protocol? Secret phrase?"

"Just an old song," Halabi replied with a sigh, indicating that she'd heard it one too many times before. "The Traffic Control Officer likes to amuse himself."

"I heard that, Lieutenant Halabi," said the voice from the speakers.

Fuseli spoke up. "This is Captain Fuseli. Stick to singing in the shower, please, and give our ship clearance to come in."

"Clearance granted," the Traffic Controller said, suddenly sounding more business-like. "Khopesh is clear for touchdown on Launch Pad 3-B."

"Got it, Base Gertrude," Rix said. "Coming in."

Fuseli sat back down in his seat and strapped himself in for their descent.

He'd seen an overhead image of Research Base Gertrude in the scant briefing materials Stroud had provided him, though now he was seeing that view for himself on the main screen and out the front window besides. The base was named after the massive crater called Gertrude, itself named after Hamlet's mother in Shakespeare's play, and at 202 miles across this crater spanned about a fifth of the moon's diameter. The base was situated within the crater itself, at a point between its rim, which was over a mile in height, and the raised area at the crater's center, which was also over a mile high.

Already Fuseli could see the three launch stations, at the ends of long tracks that branched off from the base itself like fingers from a palm. Each station consisted of four launch pads, and the stations were spaced widely apart and distant from the research area in case a ship should suffer an explosive event. Fuseli spotted two military craft of the same type as the Khopesh occupying pads, along with a nonmilitary medevac and two basic transport ships for conveying supplies or staff to and from the base. Again, these ships were distributed in such a way across the three launch stations that an explosive accident or attack would hopefully not take them all out.

The pilots of the Khopesh were bringing her down, as instructed, toward launch pad B of the third extended finger.

As they continued to descend, the lights that outlined their launch pad glowing with invitation, Fuseli took in the features of the main base area. All the various structures, like the buildings of a small frontier town, were arranged in a pentagon shape. At the center of this pentagon was a large gray dome, apparently without windows.

"I don't see any damage to the surrounding structures," Fuseli said, but he was mostly just confirming to himself what he'd already been told. "Looks like whatever went to hell was safely contained inside that dome."

"That's its purpose," Lieutenant Halabi said. "It's pretty heavily shielded."

The E.C.S. Khopesh centered itself over the designated launch pad, unfolded its landing gear as it lowered, and finally touched down. There was just a slight shudder within the cockpit as it settled. Then the landing pad's outline of lights went out...and they were here.

A collapsible docking chute was extended from a little tram station to the Khopesh, so that the patrol ship's passengers didn't have to suit up for Titania's harsh environment—which was presently minus 335 degrees Fahrenheit. Even artificial gravity was engaged, as it would be within all the base's structures, seeing as how Titania's gravity was only four percent of the Earth's.

Fuseli waited for Morris Tarragon to catch up to him so they could walk toward the Launch Station 3 tram station side-by-side through the chute. Tarragon handed Fuseli his duffel bag, then glanced back at Corporal Hoxha, who walked with several other Colonial Forcers. "I thought you jumped ship at some point," Tarragon said. "Thanks a lot for leaving me alone with Hoxha. When he saw I was awake he talked my ear off."

"You must be getting soft in your old age, putting up with that," Fuseli said.

"Now he thinks I'm his best buddy. Thanks again."

A tech and his skeletal-looking robot assistant passed them going the other way, to run the standard safety check any ship that arrived at the base had to undergo. The two pilots had remained behind, to meet with the tech when he got there. Nonmilitary, the tech nodded at Fuseli rather than saluting him as they passed each other.

"How many people on this base altogether?" Tarragon asked.

"Two hundred twenty-four, including the test subjects," Fuseli said. "Plus a dozen Bedbugs...um, Coleopteroids. That is, before the event. Now forty-one humans are dead and nine of the Coleopteroids."

"Damn."

At the end of the chute, a man of average height but sturdy build stood waiting for them with his hands on his hips, two other men standing a little behind him. All three wore Colonial Forces uniforms in the same urban color pattern Fuseli and Tarragon wore, with the two grunts additionally wearing helmets and chest armor, and carrying big Drang assault engines. The man in the fore wore a black beret instead, with only a sidearm at his hip.

"Special Ops," Tarragon noted. "That must be the head of security here."

Sure enough, when Fuseli and Tarragon reached the officer he saluted them and identified himself. "Captain Fuseli, I'm Lieutenant Rhys Tamati, head of security at Base Gertrude."

Rhys Tamati, in his early forties, was of M ori ancestry—as the *t moko* tattoos swirling across his forehead and lower face emphasized. Quite the traditional look, apart from the fact that the tattoos glowed blue like lighted filaments implanted in his skin. Along with Tamati's intense eyes and brawler's build, the tattoos made for an intimidating look, and in their field being intimidating was a positive.

Fuseli and Tarragon saluted back. "This is Lieutenant Tarragon, my personal security chief."

"I recognize the lieutenant."

"We've become notorious," Fuseli said to Tarragon.

"Not notorious, Captain—only notable," Tamati told him. "Good to meet you both."

"Likewise, Lieutenant Tamati," Fuseli said. "You going to show us around, fill us in?"

"Yes sir...at least until I introduce you to Dr. Marceau. I'll have someone stow your gear in your quarters, so I can take you right to her."

"And Dr. Marceau is the new project leader."

"Yes sir," Tamati said. "The former lead, Dr. Pulver, was one of those lost in the event. Dr. Marceau was his assistant."

Fuseli nodded. "I see."

Tamati turned, nodded to his men to get moving, then led Fuseli and Tarragon into the tram station. Here, those who had disembarked from the Khopesh and the security detail sent to greet them piled into a small tram that might have fit into the Khopesh's passenger cabin, some seated and others standing and holding onto overhead rails. Then, the tram whispered into movement, along an enclosed repulsor track. This track was one of the three extended fingers that led to the pentagon-shaped complex that was Base Gertrude itself.

Fuseli sat gazing out the tram's windows...and beyond that, through the windows of the enclosed track, at the passing moonscape of Titania. The distant sun was an almost indistinguishable glint in the sky, just another star, whereas Uranus loomed over the bleak horizon, ominously in shadow except for a crescent of ghostly blue—over twenty times larger in the sky than the Earth's moon appeared in its sky.

Fuseli knew that about twenty-three miles away lay Base Urano, the headquarters and storage facility for the Port Urano mining station in the atmosphere of Uranus. Close enough, but also safely distant in case a dangerous mishap occurred at either base: at Base Urano—though helium itself was not flammable or explosive—or due to Base Gertrude's experiments with teleportation.

Which, of course, had indeed occurred.

PART FOUR:

Research Base Gertrude

-1-

All three tram lines converged at a central station: more gritty and industrial-looking than any of the brochure-pretty tram hubs one might find at a major space station like Port Haven. Here, those who had arrived on the Khopesh and those who had come to meet them disembarked. Having been stationed at Base Gertrude in the past, Hoxha and some of the other Colonial Forcers assigned to Fuseli as security knew where to go from here, and left to show the uninitiated C-Forcers to their barracks. Fuseli saw Private Sunday glance back at him and smile as she left with the others. He nodded at her.

Along with the security team on the Khopesh had come several Port Haven engineers and techs, to aid Base Gertrude in the investigation of the disastrous event; to help repair what could be repaired, or at least salvage what could be salvaged. Mainly, to help understand what had caused it to happen in the first place. Fuseli had been introduced to these engineers prior to the flight but had already forgotten their names. Several Base Gertrude techs had been waiting in the tram hub to greet them.

Fuseli and Tarragon were left with just Tamati and his two heavily-armed companions. "So, Captain," he said, "if you'll follow me..."

There were a number of different directions to head in from the tram hub, and Tamati led them down a long narrow corridor after his wrist comp had granted them entrance to it. The two guards trailed behind Fuseli and Tarragon, silent as robots. As they walked, Fuseli looked Tamati over and said, "Forgive me for asking, Lieutenant Tamati, but you being Special Ops and all...aren't you concerned those pretty tattoos of yours might give your position away in a fight?"

Tamati looked back at Fuseli and touched a spot behind his right ear. Suddenly, the blue-glowing *t moko* tattoos were gone altogether. Tamati smiled.

"I see," Fuseli said. "Carry on."

Tamati touched that spot again and the tattoos glowed back into life.

"So what's Marceau like?" Fuseli asked him. "Not that I want to go into this with preconceived notions, but I find a lot of times Colonial Forces presence is resented by the nonmilitary operations we're supposed to watch over."

"I've stayed out of her way," Tamati said, looking back again. "So we haven't had any issues, she and I. I think she appreciates our importance here, where such a remote base could be vulnerable to pirate attacks."

"As I understand it, the pilots who brought us here have some experience dealing with pirates," Fuseli said. "How about yourself?"

"Yes, sir...I've definitely dealt with some. Not on this assignment, but when I was stationed at Port Urano we drove off a couple raiding parties. As a matter of fact, the one test subject who survived the mishap here was a pirate, himself. He was captured at Port Cygon, where he and some other Cygonese had a little gang, smuggling in illegal goods on supply ships."

The occupants of the distant starpost Port Cygon, essentially a colony in space in orbit around the ice giant Jötunn, were primarily of Vietnamese heritage. Fuseli had been there himself a number of times, most notably having stopped there for ship's repairs on his last assignment.

He fell more in step with Tamati, to speak in a graver tone. "What do you know about this prisoner's female double, or whatever she is, that teleported back from Jötunn with him? He's never been cloned by researchers here or anywhere else, has he? Maybe by someone who changed the clone's sex, as part of some other kind of experiment? Or maybe he's got a fraternal twin sister who just bears a strong resemblance to him?"

Tamati snorted a little laugh. "Sir, with all respect, don't ask me. I don't know anything about a clone of the opposite sex, but I do know the test subject's siblings are all accounted for. The ones we know of, anyway."

"Let's just say she's a previously unknown sister, or other relative. Let's even say she's a pirate, too, from that gang on Port Cygon...which, conveniently, orbits planet Jötunn. Maybe she and some other pirate buddies exploited the situation with this project here, in an attempt to help the subject escape...but in the process, this woman accidentally got sucked back here with him. In fact... it even makes me wonder if they meddled with the project in such a way that it caused the catastrophe."

"Those are all avenues to explore, sir, I'm sure, but I'm not really in a position for conjecture. You'll be wanting to confer with Dr. Marceau and the project's medical chief, Dr. Mann."

"Understood. And that I will."

-2-

A varied group of people had assembled in the research base's meeting room. Fuseli had been asked if he needed to rest first after his day-long (in Earth time) trip from Port Haven, but he assured his hosts that he wanted to at least get the ball rolling in terms of his own involvement.

Seated at the meeting table along with Fuseli, Tarragon, and the base's head of security, Tamati, were the acting head of the project, Dr. Olivia Marceau, the base's medical chief, Dr. Russell Mann, the project's chief engineer, Santosh Chawla, and the Coleopteroid Liaison.

Standing against one wall were Tamati's two armored and Drang-carrying security grunts, and on the opposite side of the room stood the only two surviving Coleopteroids besides the Liaison. Fuseli wondered if they stood behind the seated Liaison in the role of security, or simply because their chitinous bodies prevented them from sitting, too. He had never dealt with Coleopteroids in person, himself, and he tried to get a feel for whether they were resentful that nine of their team attached to the teleportation project as consultants had given their lives. However, he couldn't detect any hostility or tension from them...or any sort of emotional vibe whatsoever, for that matter. Even the Liaison, with its seemingly human face, was as unreadable as a robot. And perhaps it was one, Fuseli considered... or partly so. Better that, he thought, than what some rumored: that the heads of Coleopteroid liaisons were cloned from humans, or even worse, repurposed somehow from deceased human bodies.

Not knowing just what the Liaison consisted of, in comparison to the regular Coleopteroids, was unnerving, but the two standing Coleopteroids were typical of their extradimensional race: bipedal beetle-like entities, less than five feet in height, their bodies of glossy black chitin unclothed. They were born with three pairs of whip-like arms ending in pincers, but as was often the case, these researchers had had the lower two pairs of arms removed and replaced with a variety of complex-looking prosthetics that acted as tools or instruments, the exact purpose of which Fuseli couldn't guess. Some might even be weapons for all he knew.

In striking contrast, the Liaison had been put together in such a way as to communicate more readily with humans, and to appear more like them, no doubt with the intention of putting humans at ease. Fuseli felt the opposite effect had been achieved. Its tall, stiff body was entirely concealed within a heavy black robe, with only the head exposed. Again, this appeared to be the head of a human, devoid of hair and eyebrows, with a black metal cap bolted into the top of its head, reminding Fuseli of a yarmulke. This particular head appeared to be that of a young woman, or perhaps a teenage boy. It quickly became apparent that its eyes never blinked, and its bloodless lips barely moved when it spoke. And when it spoke, its voice was an eerie monotone, so that it sounded like a ghost come to deliver a grim message.

Given the stiffness of the Liaison's posture, and how it had seemed to float across the floor rather than walk when it had entered the meeting room, Fuseli was surprised the entity could even sit in one of the chairs arrayed around the long table.

Since the principals were all in attendance, Dr. Marceau opened things up. She was in her fifties, her brunette hair cut shortish and looking a bit mussed.

This along with her sun-deprived, somewhat gaunt face made her look as though she was going through the harshest test of her career. "I want to start off by thanking you for coming, Dr. Fuseli. I mean, Captain..."

"Either is fine," Fuseli assured her.

"You started your career as a field medic during the Gurm Conflict, I hear," Dr. Mann spoke up, leaning forward with an intrigued smile. He was in his sixties, gray-haired and rather haggard himself but with a keen, probing gaze.

"Yes," Fuseli confirmed. "Joined at eighteen. I did three years."

"My God," Mann said, wagging his head, still smiling as if at a fascinating case study. "That would definitely shape a person. You've had quite a career. Sorry to say, I haven't done any military service, myself."

Fuseli meant to stick to the topic. "In any case, I want to start off myself by offering my condolences on the loss of Dr. Pulver, and the forty other people lost in the accident. And," he nodded over at the Liaison, "the nine Coleopteroids who were lost, as well."

"We thank you for your words of respect, Dr. Fuseli," the Liaison intoned in its sepulchral voice. "Their deaths were a worthy sacrifice, considering the importance of our collaboration with your people."

"What can you tell me about the accident?" Fuseli asked, looking from the Liaison to Marceau. Then, he shifted to Mann. "And this...matter with the test subject?"

"I'll begin," Marceau said, cutting off Mann. "First off, some basic background. You'll forgive me if I cover matters you've already been briefed about..."

There were, of course, matters even more basic behind Base Gertrude's research that the project's new commander didn't even need to touch on...

At present, any manned vessel of the Earth Colonies network that embarked on interstellar travel made use of "bubble drive." This was an Alcubierre drive system that enabled faster-than-light travel by contracting space in front of the vessel (contained within its warp bubble) and expanding space behind it. To leap greater distances, however—which might take many years to traverse otherwise—the E.C. also made use of mile-long structures fixed in space called Chutes, which generated artificial wormholes for starcraft to slip into and use as shortcuts through the far reaches of space. The nearest such Chute to the Earth was one positioned between itself and Mars, and there was also a jump Chute just beyond Port Haven at the edge of Earth's solar system. These massive constructions were positioned elsewhere throughout the known regions of space, like stepping stones, helping to push exploration further and further out.

The problem was that building and powering these b-drive starcraft, and particularly the jump Chutes, was a costly business. One might very well use a Chute to reach a planet like Jötunn, and there establish an orbital spaceport like Port Cygon, but a populated colony in such an inhospitable system could only support itself so much. Sooner or later goods and new equipment needed to be shipped in, but to transport even a simple shipment of materials entailed a great expenditure of resources.

That was where the Coleopteroids came in. They were an extradimensional race, which instead of starcraft traveled between planets—and even to alternate realms of existence—by means of quantum teleportation. In the simplest of terms, their own method involved laying down a complex, overlapping system of rails like train tracks within a fairly limited area, and then driving a teleportation pod (in pictures Fuseli had seen of them, these pods reminded him of greasy old locomotive engines) along these tracks in a prescribed pattern, depending on the vehicle's destination. When the pod, dubbed a "tran," repeated this pattern a given number of times at the appropriate dizzying speed, it was warped to the destination set of tracks. This was rather like the use of jump Chutes, but expending far less energy and again enabling the tran to pass even into an alternate plane.

When the Coleopteroids had first introduced themselves to the Earth Colonies, they'd proposed an arrangement. In exchange for allowing Coleopteroid communities to settle in E.C. colonies such the one known as Punktown, on the planet Oasis, the Coleopteroids would help the E.C. develop a mode of quantum teleportation for its own use.

For reasons Fuseli didn't understand, the Coleopteroids' own method of teleportation was not suitable for human beings, or any other being but their own kind. This was why they had been working here at Base Gertrude, volunteering a top technical team to help E.C. engineers research and develop a teleportation system suitable for humans, that would enable them to transmit themselves through unfathomable distances of space...and eventually make starcraft and artificial wormholes obsolete.

Not needing to explain any of this to Fuseli, what Marceau instead laid out was the date and time of the mysterious destructive event...explaining that anomalous power surges had occurred just prior. There were ancillary research labs and support structures outside the central dome, and Marceau herself had been in one of these with Chief Engineer Chawla investigating the power surges with the two surviving Coleopteroid techs when the mishap had taken place. It was for this reason that they were alive now. Everyone within the dome itself—project leader Dr. Pulver, 40 human technicians, 9 Coleopteroid technicians, and 4 human test subjects who were waiting to be take their turns being transmitted to Jötunn and back—were killed when the explosion occurred.

"And the precise cause is still undetermined?" Fuseli interrupted.

"Yes," the head engineer Chawla replied.

"We believe we are drawing close to an answer," added the Coleopteroid Liaison.

After the explosion, Marceau continued, it was assumed that the teleportation pod, sent to the receiving research base on the planet Jötunn, would never reappear...since it had been in transit back to Base Gertrude just when systems apparently overloaded and caused the explosion. However, somehow the pod *did* eventually reappear within the blasted interior of the dome, despite the damage therein. The odd thing was, teleportation from the Jötunn base—which was manned by a sister team of researchers that included more Coleopteroids—should have only taken minutes. Instead, unaccountably, it was almost two hours before the prototype teleportation pod returned.

Just *where* the pod had been in the interim could not as yet be determined.

"When the pod was opened," Marceau went on, "the test subject was alive but unconscious inside. The pod itself was entirely intact and in itself functional... though at this point, rendered useless with so much of the equipment that could send it anywhere ruined."

"Why was he unconscious?" Fuseli asked Dr. Mann. "Had he been harmed?"

"He was found to be fine, physically, and when he came to he couldn't account for the extended period of time that had elapsed. This wasn't his first teleportation trial, and he said it didn't seem any different from those he'd experienced before."

"How could the pod decelerate on its tracks? Was the track system not ruined, too?"

The Liaison answered this. "The teleportation method we have helped design for your people does not employ a track bed, such as our own conveyances do, Dr. Fuseli. It is fixed in place."

"Okay...I see. So when the pod returned, was this unknown woman inside with the subject?"

"Not at first," Marceau said.

"Not at first?"

"I'd gone into the dome with a medical team, to get the subject out of there," Dr. Mann recounted. "To bring him to the med unit for examination. Fortunately, artificial gravity and atmospheric conditions within were maintained by equipment outside the dome. We suited up anyway, just in case, not knowing yet if conditions within might be dangerous in some other way...though we didn't read high levels of radiation. Anyway, we were transporting the subject on a stretcher, and almost out of the dome, when we heard screaming behind us. We looked back toward the open pod and saw a woman inside, looking disoriented and frantic..."

"And she wasn't in there before, but you just didn't see her when you removed the subject? Maybe she was unconscious up to that point, too."

Dr. Mann gave a chuckle that Fuseli didn't appreciate. "Dr. Fuseli, I'm sure you'll get a chance to look at the pod soon. It's quite small. There was no way we would have missed her."

"I see."

"Would you like to see the dome and the pod right now, Dr. Fuseli?" Marceau asked. "Or would you prefer to wait until you've rested a bit?"

"The trip is catching up with me," Fuseli admitted. He glanced at Tarragon, knowing his friend must feel the same. "I'll check it out later. Before I take my rest, though, I can't help but want an initial look at the test subject. And especially, this stowaway that looks like his twin sister."

"Of course," Marceau said.

"Would you like me to accompany you?" Mann said. "On the way, I can tell you—"

"If it's all right with you," Fuseli cut him off, "I'd like to see the two with fresh eyes. But if you could send your findings thus far to my wrist comp, that would be great."

Mann's smug smile had gone chilly. "Certainly. Just let me connect."

Fuseli held up the arm that wore his wrist comp, and Mann did the same, and both devices beeped as they opened a line of communication. But while Fuseli was doing this, his eyes strayed to one of the two Coleopteroids that stood against the far wall behind the seated Liaison...and not for the first time. What had drawn his attention once again was that one of this individual's lower pair of prosthetic limbs gave a distinct twitch every once in a while. Was that limb malfunctioning, or was it some kind of nervous tic? Again, Fuseli couldn't guess the purpose of that instrument, though it had an unlikely resemblance to a black chrome speculum.

Fuseli couldn't help but be fascinated with the anatomy of nonhuman beings, especially given that during his first medical stint—as a medic in the bloody Gurm Conflict—he had had to treat the wounds of humans and Gurm alike. Therefore, he noticed that both insectoid beings had little nicks and faint scratches in their chitin, which suggested to Fuseli that the conditions on their home world might be harsh, or that they lived to be quite old and had the scars to prove it. He also noticed, though, that the Coleopteroid with the twitching limb had an odd patch on one side of its head, a light gray against its otherwise obsidian-black body.

Marceau stood up from the table; the meeting appeared to be over. Fuseli lowered his wrist comp, and the project head asked, "Shall we go then, Dr. Fuseli?"

"Lead on, Dr. Marceau. But I ask one favor."

"Yes?"

"As I said to Dr. Mann, for the moment anyway I'd like observe these two from a clean perspective. Therefore, I'd like to talk with them both alone, once we get there."

Did Dr. Mann give a subdued snort? But after only meeting Fuseli's gaze for a silent second, Marceau replied, "As you wish, doctor."

-3-

Honh Yungen was certain that the snipes had followed him into that forgotten burial tunnel and killed him, after all, because when he regained consciousness it was to find himself in hell.

However, this hell was nothing like what any of the religions of his world, Sinan, threatened sinners with. There were no thousands of damned souls around him being eternally tortured and dismembered by demons of every description, the method of their punishment depending on the particular sin they had committed in life. Instead, he had found himself lying on a hard floor, like stone, with a kind of artificial jungle growing all about him, filling the mist-damp air with the rich scents of life. The most remarkable thing about this jungle—more a garden, he quickly realized—was that the vegetation was almost entirely green in color, rather than the many shades of blue he was accustomed to.

He got to his feet but remained crouching low, keeping his head below the level of a long tray beside him, in which one certain type of leafy plant was growing in neat rows. Bizarrely, these plants seemed to be growing in water or some other liquid rather than soil, and deriving their nutrients that way. Tanks of bluish fluid rested on the floor beneath the long tray, burbling as they circulated their contents.

Raising his head a little, peering out between the strange plants, Honh saw that numerous other types of plant were being grown using a variety of methods, all within a huge transparent enclosure: an immense greenhouse, large enough to contain a village. Trays like the two he crouched between, forming a kind of aisle, were stacked above each other in a dozen tiers, each tray supported by mechanical arms that could apparently rotate them out for easy access. There were also plants growing in basins on the floor against the greenhouse's walls, and in racks of fixed shelving, and even in odd rings or hoops arranged vertically with a light source at their center, perhaps meant to minimize the amount of floor space required. Meanwhile, a series of narrow clear cases, filed vertically as if in a bookcase, appeared to be growing algae inside them, which he assumed to be edible. All the plants being grown, regardless of their type: beautifully, fantastically green. Though, Honh did see what appeared to be colored fruits or vegetables in the mix.

At the center of the greenhouse he noted a large circular tank in which fish were swimming, though from here Honh couldn't tell how alike or unalike they were to fish he was familiar with. He assumed they were being raised to be eaten, like the plants. Also, from across the open space came the distinct chirping of insects, and unless they infested the plants—which Honh doubted, seeing how carefully maintained this interior farm was—he figured the insects were kept in enclosures he couldn't see from this angle, being raised as a food source, too.

Even more disorienting than the green vegetation, though, was what Honh saw through the transparent panes that made up the hemispherical covering of the great greenhouse. It was apparently night out there, the sky aglitter with stars, but this was surely not night on his world of Sinan. Firstly, the landscape looked utterly barren and frozen...and Honh had only ever seen photographs of his world's ice caps; he'd never himself set foot in an icy region. But even more alien than this: out there hung a monstrous blue crescent moon that blacked out a shocking amount of the starry sky. Or...was *this* the moon of *that* world?

Whichever it was, Honh was finally realizing that he wasn't in hell...but somehow on another world than his own.

So, had he been reincarnated here? He could rule that out immediately. Not only was he in an adult body, but his *own* adult body. See? On the tops of his hands were the old, faded symbols he'd had tattooed there when he was nineteen, to give himself better luck in gambling. Plus, he was still wearing the same clothes he had worn when out checking his traps earlier today (if it *was* the same day). He had even awoken with his prized hunting rifle clutched in his right hand.

Wherever he was, he didn't understand how he'd come to be here, and it terrified him almost to the point of panic. He was shaking so badly that he might as well have been out there in that frozen landscape itself, and he had all he could do to stop himself from whimpering aloud.

He turned in his crouch to look behind him, through the windows on the other side of the greenhouse. Though tiers of trays loaded with plants stood between him and those windows, he could still see other structures out there in the stark night. Dominating them was a large dark dome, blocking out an area of star-flecked sky like another planet looming on the horizon. The great humped dome had no windows, apparently, but a few marker beacons flashed on it to perhaps alert flying craft to its presence.

The dome held his gaze for a while, as if it should mean something to him... if only he could remember why.

Honh became aware of a whirring sound approaching, and he whipped his head toward it, bringing his rifle up in both hands. The sound, though not loud in itself, grew more pronounced. Something appeared to be entering the aisle on the other side of this tray in front of him. Honh crouched a bit lower, peering out through the plants as if lying in wait for his prey back home...be it animal or fellow Sinanese.

The source of the soft whirring came into view behind the screen of leaves. It was a mobile machine, like a self-driving cart, its body largely consisting of a clear tank of that same blue-tinted solution that filled the tanks feeding the rows of plants. At the cart's front, though, was an upright section that was vaguely anthropomorphic, with a variety of insect-like limbs and a kind of head with glowing blue eyes.

Honh was only familiar with such fanciful automatons from bedtime stories and children's movies, but he recognized it for what it was. The question was, how sentient was the thing...and did it have anything to do with his presence here? Had it and its mechanical brethren captured him somehow, and brought him here to be a slave in this strange garden of plenty? But if that were the case, who was the food being grown for, except the slaves themselves?

Maybe Honh had gasped, or made some other involuntary sound, or perhaps the automaton had caught a glimpse of him crouching behind the tray. Whatever the case, the thing suddenly stopped advancing along the aisle on the other side of the tray and its head, such as it was, swiveled in his direction. He felt the gaze of its glowing eyes.

"Excuse me...who are you? What are you doing here?"

It wasn't the machine that had uttered these words in a language Honh didn't understand, but rather a person who had entered the aisle when Honh's horrified eyes had been glued to the automaton. Startled, Honh sprang to his feet, whirled toward the voice, and fired his hunting rifle.

The woman he'd shot through the chest, whom he judged to be older than himself, was both beautiful and grotesque to his eyes...in that her flesh was not blue, but a strange pale pinkish color. Her eyes, though, bulging in shock and pain, were an eerie blue. At least her blood was red, as it ran from the wound in her chest and where it had sprayed from the greater hole blown out her back.

With the woman still staring at Honh in horror, essentially dead on her feet, she collapsed to the floor in front of him.

Without waiting to see how the automaton might react, what weapons it might produce, Honh whipped toward it and fired a second shot. He heard the clunk of metal but wasn't sure he had punctured the thing or inflicted any real damage. He didn't wait to find out. Without knowing how he might escape from this alien world he had been forced into—nor even how he might escape this room—he simply plunged blindly ahead into the orderly green jungle.

4

While there were no prison cells, as such, at Base Gertrude, the five test subjects had been given quarters in a little wing built off the general crew barracks. When not personally involved in the testing—or having their bodies examined and vital systems monitored following teleportation runs—the convicts had been free to roam the base, but only as a group and accompanied by at least one member of security. During rest hours, they had been locked in their individual rooms.

It was toward these rooms that Fuseli went now, accompanied by Tarragon, Security Chief Tamati, Dr. Marceau, and Dr. Mann. While they walked the base's corridors, connecting one structure to another, Marceau filled Fuseli and Tarragon in on more details about the base as a whole.

Because shipping large amounts of building materials from Earth or even some close colony would have been impractical and expensive, much of the base components had been created right here on Titania, three-dimensionally printed using the moon's own resources for material. However, the Coleopteroids had also provided certain exotic materials and a good deal of equipment, and that had had to be transported on cargo vessels from Earth, where the Coleopteroids had been permitted to establish their own teleportation base so as to access this plane. In turn, those materials had been teleported to the Earth from a facility on the Coleopteroids' own extradimensional world...to which no human being had ever traveled.

Marceau went on to explain how H2O was also derived from the moon's water ice, with the water then undergoing electrolysis to split it into hydrogen and oxygen to help support the base's breathable atmosphere. Further, hydrogen could be combined with carbon monoxide to create hydrocarbon fuels to help support the base's energy needs.

"Every approach in conjunction helps support the whole," Marceau said. "But I'm sure much of this stuff is already familiar to you. Anyway, since we don't know how long we'll be here conducting our research, we've tried to make this base as self sufficient as possible. Until we're ready to reproduce the teleportation system safely on Earth or elsewhere, we could be here for years...especially after this terrible setback."

"Well, you do look pretty self sustaining," Fuseli said. "From above, I saw you have an impressive hydroponics setup."

"That was a must," Marceau said. "We grow a good variety of foodstuffs, from conventional terrestrial vegetables to edible algae produced in high-yield micro farms. Not to mention, we raise some tasty fish and crickets! And of course, we're outfitted with the usual food fabricators that work with fermented bacteria. Like I say...every approach in conjunction."

"The bottom line is, we won't starve here anytime soon," Mann said, patting his rounded belly. "Whatever other disasters have befallen us."

They came at last to the barracks subdivision where the convicts-turned-volunteers had been housed. Now only one of them remained, though the mysterious woman had been given a room formerly occupied by one of the deceased.

"This is where I'd like to go in alone...just for the first look," Fuseli said.

"I was hoping you'd change your mind by the time we got here," Mann said.

"And here I thought you just wanted to share a stroll with me, Dr. Mann."

Mann smiled thinly. "I thought it might be interesting and perhaps revealing to see how the woman responds to your interview, Dr. Fuseli...but whatever method works best for you. Though in my experience, collaboration always achieves the best results."

"I won't dispute that, but as I've said, I just want to eyeball these two for a few minutes before I go and have me a nice nap."

"Understood, Doctor...understood."

"Well then," Marceau said, "Dr. Mann and I will leave you with Lieutenant Tamati, who can show you to your quarters afterwards. Sorry to say they're also two rooms formerly occupied by test subjects, right here next door. We're at a shortage for guest accommodations, as I'm sure you understand."

"Not a problem at all, Dr. Marceau. Just don't lock me in at night, if you don't mind."

Marceau smiled. "I promise." She nodded at Fuseli and Tarragon before starting away. "Then we'll talk again soon, Dr. Fuseli."

"We will. Thank you, Dr. Marceau...Dr. Mann."

Mann grunted, and followed Marceau back the way they had come. When they'd turned a corner, Mann throwing one last sour look back at them, Fuseli turned to Tamati and said, "I want to have a look at the man first. I'll save our mystery woman for after."

"I know you don't want your observations of them influenced by other people's impressions, sir, but I've got to say...you may not like her much."

"I don't expect to like the man, either," said Fuseli. "But then, I'm not a fan of pirates."

"Sir, if I might ask...are you not liking Dr. Mann's vibe?"

"It's not so much that. I'm not trying to be a dick, here, but this is my investigation so I need to mark my territory a bit."

Tamati smiled, nodded, gestured for them to proceed.

As they stepped toward the door to the test subject's quarters, Tarragon whispered to Fuseli, "Not trying to be a dick, huh?"

"Actually, I'm trying to be the bigger dick," Fuseli said. "But hey, I've got a job to do."

At present there was no guard in this wing to make sure the test subject didn't get up to any mischief, and there were no longer any other test subjects for the man to visit in their rooms or vice versa, so his door was kept locked. Tamati unlocked it, the door slid aside, and he announced their presence.

"Tony Nguyen...you got guests."

Tamati gestured for Fuseli to enter, and remained just outside the open door while Fuseli and Tarragon stepped into what was more a walk-in closet than a room, accommodating only its tenant's cot-like bed and a little flip-down desk with a single chair, though multiple storage cupboards were set into the walls.

The man sat on the edge of his bed, watching them without getting up to greet them, having just shut off the movie he'd been watching on a wall screen. He wore a bright yellow top and pants like surgical scrubs, and Fuseli noted the tracker band locked around one ankle. Fuseli knew the man was of Vietnamese ancestry, and he looked younger than his forty years, handsome with his hair gelled back like a movie star and his scruffy little mustache and goatee. His gaze on Fuseli was like that of a leopard behind the bars of its cage.

Fuseli removed his black greatcoat, folded it onto the desk and then placed his beret atop it. He turned the only chair to face the bed and sat down, while Tarragon remained standing against one wall, towering with his hands in his greatcoat's pockets.

"So, Anthony Nguyen," Fuseli said. "I'm Captain Robert Fuseli."

"Yeah," Nguyen said. "They told me you were coming. Is the military taking over this operation, then?"

"The Colonial Forces always support any Earth Colonies venture." Fuseli pointed to a purplish port-wine stain on the left side of the man's face, around his pronounced cheekbone. "You know a vascular birthmark like that is easy to remove?"

"And?" Nguyen said. "Maybe I like looking like I just came out of a fight."

Fuseli then nodded at the little gold cross the man wore around his neck. "Anthony, huh? You a good Christian?"

"My mom gave me this. She was a Catholic."

"Was?"

"She passed away. My dad's still alive. He works in a warehouse on Port Cygon."

"So you didn't follow your dad's example of making an honest living, huh?"

Nguyen snorted. "At his age, he should be retired by now instead of breaking his back every day. And my mom should still be alive running her little pho place, but she worked almost up to the day she died. So much for honest living."

Nguyen's hands were clasped between his spread legs, and Fuseli noted there were the halves of a yin and yang tattooed on their tops: a black half on his right hand, a white half on the left. Fuseli gestured at them. "Are you a Buddhist or something on top of being a Christian?"

"I'm neither." Nguyen held up his hands. "These just mean that nothing is ever in balance. Nothing is ever whole. It's all just broken."

"What a depressing outlook. Anyway, so you'd been given a twenty-year sentence for your pirate gang activities, but volunteering for this program reduced it to ten. Still a good stretch, but better than twenty. You might still turn your life around when you're done."

"Yeah...sure. Count on it."

"And they gave you a chunk of money, too, I understand. You holding onto that for when you're free, or did you give it to your dad?"

"He wouldn't take it. We don't talk anymore. I have two brothers in Port Cygon and a sister on Earth. I split it up between them."

"That's commendable. So...I want to ask you a few questions about your experiences, until more questions occur to me and we talk again."

"Go for it."

"The day of the accident was your fourth time traveling in that teleportation pod, to and from?"

"Yes."

"Did that experience seem different to you in any way from the first three times? Any different physical sensations, or did you even just have a different feeling about it?"

"I didn't notice anything different than before. The experience is a hard thing to describe. While the power is building up, and your body is getting scanned or whatever those Bedbugs do, you feel jittery...anxious...but that could all just be psychological. Once you actually teleport, well, you're not really conscious of *moving* anywhere. It feels pretty much instantaneous. I guess I might say that right before it happens, it feels like your body is about to explode in a billion pieces, in a billion directions at once, but that might just be psychological, too. Next thing you know, you're whole on the other side."

"I thought you said nothing is ever whole."

Nguyen narrowed his hooded eyes. "As whole as I can ever be. Of course, the thing about teleporting is you get destroyed in the process. What appears on the other side is basically an exact replica. Know what I mean? So I guess I'm currently on my eighth version of 'me.'"

"Well," Fuseli said, "considering how many cells of our bodies we naturally replace during our lifetime, I guess we never stay the same 'me' physically. You ever hear of the Ship of Theseus? It's a philosophical question about identity. The concept is, if you replace every board in a boat over time, is it still the same boat?"

"That raises the question...if I'm a different 'me,' should I still have to serve ten years for crimes an earlier 'me' committed?"

Fuseli smiled. "Try that one in court. Moving right along, did you ever lose consciousness while teleporting?"

"Only on the ride back from the Jötunn base, right as the accident was happening. I guess that's why I blacked out, but who knows? Seems they still haven't figured out all the whys yet about what happened. Anyway, other than that, I did puke in my lap the very first time I ported."

"On the way back from Jötunn that last time, did you know there was a woman in the pod with you?"

"There *was* no woman in the pod with me at that time. There would have been no place for her to hide. Thing's smaller than this room."

"Do you have friends or family on Jötunn, Tony Nguyen? Namely...pirate friends?"

"You think pirates could sneak somebody into that pod with me?"

"Maybe a pirate could infiltrate the research team. Either on Jötunn or maybe even here."

"And do what?"

"Maybe sabotage the experiment to free you somehow?"

"Free me *how?* By teleporting me to some secret pirate teleportation base instead? Come on, Captain."

"You ever been cloned, Tony Nguyen?"

"Cloned? What are you on about now? You mean the woman? She's...a *woman.*"

"A man can undergo procedures..."

"Are you for real, Captain? So you think I was cloned and my clone had a sex change?"

"Have you seen this woman yourself? They say she looks just like you."

"Racists might think all Vietnamese look alike. But yeah, okay, she does look like me. They won't let me meet her, but I've seen her accidentally a couple times in passing."

"You said you have a sister."

"She's on Earth, I said...you can check. And she's six years younger than me... not to mention like six inches shorter than me."

"Any other sisters? Maybe one that isn't on record?"

"*No.* Look...I don't know who this girl is. They won't even tell me her name! Why is that? And why won't they let me meet her?"

"I didn't know they hadn't told you her name, but I imagine they want to keep you two separate so they can make sure there's no collusion. No putting your heads together to get your stories straight."

"Stories straight. Jesus Christ," Nguyen huffed. "Look, Captain Whoever... when they pulled that girl out of the pod I was already blacked out and on my way to the med unit. I never saw her during teleportation because she didn't start out in the pod with me. You think all those researchers and techs and whatnot on

Jötunn wouldn't have seen her get in? She didn't teleport back here *with* me...she teleported here *after* me."

Fuseli leaned back in his chair and sighed, digesting all this. He glanced behind him at Tarragon, who'd stood there silent and unmoving all this time, then faced Nguyen again. "It's been a long day, so I'll be going over here to my quarters next door to catch some rest. If you can think of anything else to share with me, any details you remember or impressions you had, you can buzz for security and they'll let me know."

"We will," Tamati concurred, outside the door.

"With that whole laboratory ruined, they're going to have to start again from scratch," Nguyen said, "if they don't scrap the project altogether. Have you heard them say whether they're going to keep me on here as a lab rat, or tell me I've fulfilled my duty and send me back to prison?"

"Where's prison for you?"

"Prison's on that fucking ice ball Jötunn, too."

"They haven't told me what's to be done with you later on, but for now I want you here until I have more answers about that woman."

"Why don't you ask *her* who she is and how she got into that pod?"

Fuseli stood from the little chair and retrieved his coat and beret. "That's my next stop before my nap."

-5-

Honh Yungen had stumbled out from between the tiers of plant-laden trays to find himself in a wider central aisle that ran the entire length of the greenhouse. Lamps mounted above, simulating sunlight, blazed down like spotlights as if to reveal him.

There were doors out of the greenhouse at either end, though he didn't know where they might lead to. And did he really want to get outside, where conditions appeared to be frigid? But he was in a panic, and closer to one of the two exits than the other, so this was the one he bolted for.

Just as Honh was nearing the door, a figure stepped out into the aisle just ahead of him. Even as he skidded to a halt and brought his rifle up again, he saw that it was another automaton...though this one was superficially more human-like than the first, in that it at least had two legs to walk on and only two arms, one of them carrying a tool box or the like. Again, empty blue-glowing eyes turned on him. Might those eyes shoot killing beams of light, as in the movies children enjoyed? Honh didn't wait to find out. Having shouldered the rifle for a better aim, he fired directly at the machine-man's head.

The automaton was struck and staggered back a step, but remained on its feet. One of its eyes had gone dark. The thing didn't advance at him, but neither did it try to flee to avoid another shot. It didn't seem to know how to process the situation, but there it stood, between Honh and the exit, so he turned away and fled down the central aisle toward the farther exit.

As he ran, Honh counted off the shots he had already taken. One for the strangely-colored woman, and one each for the two automatons. That left just two bullets in his clip before he would have to reload his rifle.

Just as with the door the machine-man had blocked, intentionally or otherwise, Honh saw no latch or knob on the door at the far end, but there was a panel with glowing buttons to one side of the door that he hoped would allow him to open it.

Even as he was considering how much ammo he had left, and how he might open that door once he reached it, the door slid open (instead of swinging open on hinges as he had expected) to reveal a figure standing in the threshold: a man with dark brown skin this time, wearing a uniform similar to the pinkish-skinned woman.

Honh came to an abrupt stop once again, he and the brown-skinned man locking eyes, and brought up his rifle...

But before Honh could fire, the man ducked back around the edge of the doorway and apparently did something on his side to shut the door again, because it slid back into its closed position.

Honh was left there in the aisle as if hanging by his fingertips over a chasm, trapped between the automaton at one end and, at the other, a man who was aware of his presence, no doubt lying in wait behind the closed door. Not knowing what else to do, Honh hissed a curse and plunged back into the artificial jungle...

to look for perhaps a third way out of this enclosure. And all the while, the blue rim of that gigantic dark world hanging in the sky beyond the greenhouse panes stared in at him like the slitted eye of an alien god.

"Who are you, now?" the woman demanded, before Fuseli could even introduce himself.

Like Anthony Nguyen, the woman wore bright yellow scrubs, and they'd even put a tracker around one of her ankles, too. She had taken her shoes off, and she'd been reclining on her bed in a tiny room identical to Nguyen's watching a program on the wall screen when Tamati unlocked the room for Fuseli and Tarragon to enter.

As before, Fuseli set his coat and beret down on the little flip-down desk and took a seat, while Tarragon loomed nearby like a glowering totem.

"I'm Captain Robert Fuseli...a medical officer with the Colonial Forces," Fuseli replied amicably. "And your name is?"

"How many times do I have to tell you people?" the woman all but snarled. "My name hasn't changed since you first asked me. It's Rhan Luyen."

"Okay...nice to meet you, Rhan."

"Maybe *you* can tell me why I'm a prisoner here."

"You're not a prisoner, Rhan...we just want to understand how it is that you came here, and in the meantime we want to keep you safe."

"Just keeping me safe, huh? Is that why I have to buzz for a guard every time I need to use the toilet?" Rhan Luyen snorted. "Well, I'd like to understand how I came to be here, myself."

To Fuseli, Nguyen's voice hadn't sounded any more accented than his own, but this woman had a slight accent of some kind. That wasn't the only difference between herself and the former pirate, but there weren't many, aside from the two being of biologically opposite sexes. Rhan's hair fell just to her collar, and the contours of her face were softer than Nguyen's, but she too was apparently about forty (while looking younger, like him), and she had the same fierce, penetrating eyes under intense brows. Fuseli found the woman as intimidating as she was beautiful, and that intrigued him. He wasn't easily intimidated.

Fuseli pointed to the port-wine stain that peeked out from her hair and spread onto her left cheekbone. "Did you hurt yourself?" he asked innocently.

Rhan touched her face. "This? I thought you said you're a doctor. I was born with this. What, you think I'm ugly?"

"Hardly." Fuseli's gaze shifted to her hands, looking for tattoos. She didn't have any. He asked, "Where did you live before coming here? On Jötunn?"

"I've said before...I don't know any place called Jötunn. And no, not that Port Cygon you people keep asking me about, either."

"You'll have to forgive me; I just arrived on Titania so I'm not sure what exactly you've already gone over with Dr. Mann and the others."

"That Dr. Mann is a pervert. He keeps finding any excuse to get me out of my clothes to check me out."

"I don't rule out that he's a pervert, but he is a doctor, too, you know. So...if not Jötunn or Port Cygon, where do you come from?"

"I live in Gosston."

"Gosston? Where is that?"

"On Earth."

From the open doorway, Tamati spoke up. "Captain Fuseli? We've looked into her claim. There is no city or town on Earth named Gosston."

"Whatever you say, chief," Rhan snapped.

"Have they run a truth scan on her?" Fuseli asked Tamati.

"Not sure, sir."

"We'll want to do that. I have the program on my wrist comp." Fuseli faced Rhan again. "Have you lived in this Gosston all your life?"

"No. My parents moved us there from the country where I was born."

"Okay, and what country was that?"

"Like I've said, my country doesn't have a name, officially."

"Ah...come again?"

Rhan heaved a disgusted sigh, and swung her sock-clad feet off her bed to sit up on its edge. "The story is, ages ago the great Emperor Tho decided to hide my country from outsiders so they'd stop trying to invade us. And supposedly, to keep demons from finding us, too, and plaguing my country with bad luck. So, Emperor Tho stripped my country of whatever name it used to have and forbade folks from using it. So today, my country is only known as the Unnamed Country."

"The...Unnamed Country. Okay."

"Gonna need that truth scan," Tarragon rumbled.

"You go ahead and do that," Rhan said. "I'm not afraid. You think the things you've been telling me are any less crazy? That we're on some moon of the seventh planet in the solar system? That you're working on some magic machine that can disassemble people here and reassemble them on some other planet light-years away?"

"Not only do you not live on Jötunn, then, but you've never traveled there?" Fuseli asked. "Or any other planet, aside from the Earth?"

"No! Of course not...and no one else has, either. Except for the moon. I mean...I haven't been to the moon, but other people have."

Fuseli and Tarragon looked at each other, then Fuseli faced Rhan again. "What year is this, for you?"

"For me? It's 2023."

Tamati mumbled something from the doorway.

"How do you account for being where you are now, then?" Fuseli asked her. "Any ideas? And by the way, have you been able to look out any windows lately? If so, it should be apparent you're not on the Earth."

"How can I be sure those windows aren't all video screens or something like that? How can I even be sure I'm awake right now, and not drugged up as part of some crazy experiment? After all, I keep hearing about all these weird experiments going on here."

"So you don't know how you ended up in that teleportation pod?"

"No! I woke up in that thing and it freaked me out."

"What's the last thing you remember before you woke up in there?"

"I was at work, in Gosston. It's a company that makes prosthetics..."

"Medical prosthetics?"

"*Yes*, medical prosthetics! I work in shipping and receiving, and the warehouse. I was feeling weird, like dizzy or something. I thought I was just tired, because I'm always tired on the night shift. I went into the ladies' room to sit down on the toilet for a minute. I got really faint or something and put my head down between my knees so I wouldn't pass out, but I guess I did, because the next thing I knew I'm waking up in that pod thing. Inside that dome it was all burnt, with smoke and the smell of burning plastic and whatever, and that's why I freaked out so much at first: I thought the factory was on fire. And then these hands are dragging me out of the pod..."

"Interesting," Fuseli said.

"You think?"

"The man in the next cell...uh, room over here..."

"So I'm not a prisoner, huh?"

"Sorry. Anyway, what can you tell me about him?"

"Not much, except he looks like he came from my country."

"That being, this...Unnamed Country."

"Yes. But they won't let me meet him, and they won't even tell me his name. What's up with that, Captain Whoever?"

"That's funny, you calling me that. He called me Captain Whoever, too."

"Well, who is he?"

"You haven't seen him?"

"Only in passing a couple times."

"Did you think he resembles you, Rhan? As in, very closely?"

"I didn't see him well, but yeah, like I said, he looks like he comes from the same place I do."

Behind them, just outside the doorway, Security Chief Rhys Tamati got a call on his wrist comp. He stepped away a little so as not to interrupt the interview as he answered, but Fuseli turned to listen anyway...and grew more interested when he heard Tamati's voice become excited.

"Who is it doing the shooting?" Tamati cried.

From here, Fuseli couldn't hear the person who was calling very well. "What's going on?" he asked.

"Send people over there immediately!" Tamati said. "Block both entrances, and have a team go inside to subdue the shooter!"

Fuseli stood up from the desk's little chair. "Who has guns in this place besides security?"

Tamati had ended his call. "No one, sir. With your permission..."

"Yes, go—and I'm coming with you." Fuseli nodded at Tarragon. "You, too."

"Of course." Tarragon was already pulling his sidearm: a standard-issue Scythe .55 with an internal silencing feature. Who knew what they might encounter on the way to wherever this shooting was?

Before leaving the room, Fuseli looked back at Rhan Luyen and said, "We'll talk again, Rhan."

"Good luck, Captain Whoever."

-6-

Except for the trams that shuttled crew and supplies to and from the three launch stations, Base Gertrude didn't have any trams that connected the structures arrayed around the central dome. Even if one was immediately at hand, driving to the hydroponics greenhouse in one of the base's little carts wouldn't have gotten them there much faster, so Tamati, Fuseli, and Tarragon ran through various corridors and sections of the base to get there.

As they ran, Tamati communicated with one of his people, who was stationed in the security office. "What do the security cameras show?" he huffed.

"We've reviewed the vid," came a voice from Tamati's wrist comp. "The shooter's killed one woman in there and fired on two robots. We've lost sight of him now...he's hiding back in all the plants, out of camera range. Last seen around the greenhouse midpoint."

"Can you identify him?"

"A male with blue skin."

"Blue *skin?*"

Fortunately it wasn't far from the barracks to hydroponics, and they were already coming up on one of the doors into the greenhouse. Outside the door were stationed three security guards wearing helmets and body armor over their camos, Drang assault engines gripped in their fists. Drangs were bulky-looking but fairly lightweight, boasting three muzzles from which one could choose to fire solid projectiles, energy bolts, or grenades.

"We've got three people on the other door, too," one of Tamati's people reported, "and three have gone inside."

"Okay," Tamati said, touching the spot behind his ear to make his blue-glowing facial tattoos disappear. "I'm going in, too."

"Us, too," said Fuseli.

"Captain..."

"Forget who we are, Lieutenant?" Fuseli turned to ask the guard who'd reported, "Any other workers in there?"

"No, sir, just robots now."

"Let's do it," Tamati said, reaching out to activate the door control. "Seal it up after us."

"Yes sir." The guard spoke into his helmet mic. "Don't get trigger-happy in there...the chief and two others are coming in."

The door whisked open and Tamati darted out of the doorway quickly to let Fuseli and Tarragon follow, all three of them now with their Scythe handguns drawn. The door slid shut again behind them and locked.

The three Special Ops officers took cover behind one of those twelve-tiered racks of planted vegetation. Using sign language, Tamati indicated he was going to cross to the right side of the greenhouse to search for the shooter. Fuseli signaled back that he and Tarragon would check the left side. Then, Tamati broke cover and ran, and Fuseli nodded to Tarragon and they started down the length of the greenhouse, sticking to the aisle closest to the lefthand wall. Beyond the panes that made up the hydroponics enclosure, the crescent of Uranus looked on at the drama with cold detachment, perhaps amused that a greenhouse existed so far from the light of any sun. As they moved along, Fuseli and Tarragon were careful to check under the trays, where aquarium-like tanks of nutrient solution on the floor burbled softly.

Fuseli paused to whisper to Tarragon. "Let me know if you spot the shooter's victim. She might not really be dead. If we find her, I'll stay with her."

"Got it."

They continued on ahead for a bit, then paused to poke their heads up from their crouch. Several aisles to their right, Fuseli spotted two Colonial Forces soldiers creeping along, checking opposite sides of the aisle they were in, their Drangs held ready for action. From her profile, Fuseli recognized one of them as Private Amaka Sunday, who'd accompanied him on the Khopesh.

The other Colonial Forcer, looking this way and that, turned and caught Fuseli watching them. Their eyes met, and Fuseli saw it was his talkative friend Corporal Alban Hoxha. Hoxha smiled and nodded, and a shot boomed and half of Hoxha's face was smashed in. He dropped back out of sight behind all the intervening trays of plants.

"Fuck!" Fuseli cried, standing up and looking toward the area he thought the shot had come from.

Amaka whipped in that direction, too, firing a burst of solid projectiles from her Drang. The gun's chatter was deceptively subdued, but bits of shredded plants jumped up and projectiles whined as they ricocheted off the greenhouse panes, which were thankfully too sturdy to be shattered.

Fuseli heard a shriek of pain from somewhere up ahead of him, where Amaka had strafed back and forth with her Drang before ducking down out of sight, presumably beside Hoxha.

"Come out!" Fuseli shouted. "Put your weapon down and give yourself up!" He was moving in the direction of that cry he'd heard. And then, a voice answered him...screaming words that he couldn't make out. It wasn't just pain that made it impossible to understand them. They seemed to be in a language Fuseli couldn't identify.

Tamati came running, and the other of the three grunts who had gone in before them. They and Fuseli and Tarragon all pretty much converged on the shooter at the same time.

The man lay half under one of the long trays, where apparently he'd been hiding between two nutrient tanks. Several of Amaka's bullets had punched through his chest, and he was splayed on his back wheezing, one lung punctured, his eyes wide with horror as he stared up at the faces that hung over him. Tarragon kicked the man's rifle away from his hand, then stooped down to pick it up and examine it as if it were some curious artifact.

"Jesus Christ," said Tamati. "Look at his face."

The man babbled piteously, between the wheezing and the gurgling of blood in his throat.

"What's that language?" Tarragon said. "Not Vietnamese."

Amaka came bursting through all the edible foliage to join them, with Hoxha's blood on her hands. She pointed her Drang down at the dying man's face and snarled through gritted teeth, "He killed Alban!"

Fuseli gently pushed her Drang to point away from the man she'd shot. "I know, Private."

"Can we save him?" Tarragon asked, even as Tamati was on his wrist comp to Dr. Mann, asking him to send medics.

The blue-skinned man, who they would never know had been called Honh Yungen in life, gave a last rattling gurgle and went still, his eyes locked open and a tear rolling down his cheek.

"No," Fuseli said.

Fuseli watched the tear dribble across an irregular splotch on the dead man's left cheek, the birthmark a darker blue again his blue skin.

Tarragon wagged his head in awe. "It's the same guy, isn't it? Only blue this time."

Fuseli could only grunt, still staring at the dead man's face. Aside from the blue skin, he had the exact same features as Anthony Nguyen, the sole survivor of the teleportation mishap...right down to the scruffy little mustache and goatee. Not to mention, though the designs were different, this man also had tattoos on the tops of both hands.

"Maybe Tony Nguyen did get cloned, after all," Tamati said, finished with his call for medics. "But this clone dyed his skin?"

"His skin isn't dyed," Fuseli said. And then: "Get back." He himself stood up quickly and backed away from the body a few steps. The others did the same.

Where one of the bullets had struck the blue-skinned man in the heart, wisps of black gas came twisting up out of the wound. Fuseli was concerned the thick vapor might be the result of some toxic medical condition, or perhaps even a hidden weapon the man had triggered before dying, but in no time the black gas began to thin out and dissipate.

"Needless to say, I want a post mortem on this guy," Fuseli said. "And I want to talk to the Coleopteroid Liaison."

-7-

In Base Gertrude's med unit, the dead man lay unclothed on an examination table. In the bright overhead lights the cleaned wounds in his chest stood out neatly, like peepholes into a dark and enigmatic other place. His eyes were closed now, his expression in death composed.

Standing over him, Dr. Russell Mann said to Fuseli, "I've scanned him thoroughly, and recorded him for posterity, Dr. Fuseli, so if you don't object I'd like to actually cut into him."

Standing on the other side of the table, acting project director Dr. Olivia Marceau protested, "Is that really necessary? Shouldn't we preserve him intact, in case we never encounter a being like this again? Especially given that he's a human-type being, when we've encountered so few of them!"

Fuseli said, "I'd want to do the same as Dr. Mann. Nothing like getting your hands in there." He faced Mann. "Permission granted. What does the scan say about him genetically, in relation to Nguyen and the woman?"

"Obviously, not having come from the same fertilized egg, they don't share the same DNA," Mann replied, "but they do share very similar genetic makeups, more like fraternal twins. Even with this fellow here not being a human of Earth origin."

Now Fuseli turned to the Coleopteroid Liaison, who also stood over the examination table, its face as expressionless as ever. Who could really say what went on behind those unblinking eyes? The Liaison looked every bit as dead as the cadaver lying before it.

"And what do you say?" Fuseli asked it. "Have your people ever encountered a being like this before in your travels?"

"Not to my knowledge," said the Liaison in its ghostly voice. "Though, I am not in a position to discuss matters that do not apply directly and exclusively to the research we are conducting here."

"Oh, is that right?" Fuseli said. "Can you at least confirm that you're not familiar with this type of being?"

"As I say, Dr. Fuseli, not to the best of my knowledge. I am not privy to all the information my people have gathered in their explorations."

"How would you account for the uncanny resemblance this alien being shares with the test subject Anthony Nguyen and this woman, Rhan Luyen?"

"I could only offer a theory," the Liaison said.

"Can I offer you my theory, to see if they're similar?" Fuseli said. "I propose that the three individuals in question are essentially the same individual."

"*Yes!*" hissed Dr. Mann, grinning. "This is my theory, as well!"

"What are you saying?" Dr. Marceau exclaimed.

"I believe I must also concur," the Liaison said. "These two alien beings appear to be alternate versions of the man named Anthony Nguyen."

"Have you ever experienced a phenomenon like this before?" Fuseli asked it.

"I have not personally, prior to this."

"I don't mean *personally*...I mean your people. Have your people ever encountered alternate versions of themselves, or any other beings in the course of extra-dimensional travel?"

"As I have said, Doctor, I am not at liberty—"

"God damn it," Fuseli said. "Why so secretive, all of a sudden?"

"I am simply following protocols, Doctor."

"But you say you concur, about what's happening here."

"Yes. Though I cannot as yet explain how this has come to be, except to state the obvious. This must have come about as a consequence of the accident in the research lab."

"But this man didn't come out of the teleportation pod, too, did he?" Marceau said. "We have guards outside the door."

Tamati was present, though standing back a bit from the table, and he said, "We're looking at vids from all the base's security cameras, but so far we haven't seen this guy anywhere except in the greenhouse. Looks like somehow he materialized in there, but if he did, it must've been in a spot where the cameras didn't have an unobstructed view."

"How is that possible?" Marceau said.

"How indeed?" said Fuseli.

"But the equipment we've developed is for teleportation within our own universe...not between different universes."

"Nevertheless," the Liaison said, "the technology we've assisted you with is much the same as what my people use for extra-dimensional teleportation, and so there is a strong likelihood that extra-dimensional teleportation was accidentally achieved."

"But why would the woman appear in the pod, and yet this man seems to have appeared in the greenhouse?"

"As yet, I have no idea, Dr. Marceau," said the Liaison. "Rest assured, we will be investigating this matter ourselves...here, and at the Jötunn base, and on our home world as soon as I file my report."

Fuseli glanced across the med unit, where the only other two surviving Coleopteroid researchers stood in front of a wall into which a row of cryogenic life support chambers were set. The bodies of the murdered hydroponics worker and Corporal Alban Hoxha had been stored in two of those cryo drawers. There were no other bodies in them, despite the great loss of life from the explosion in the research lab, since those victims had all been blasted apart or burned to cinders. What remains had been gathered had all been properly incinerated, though it was impossible to sort through the ashes to send those of individuals home to loved ones.

Once again, Fuseli noted how one of the multiple prosthetic limbs of one of the two beetle-like Coleopteroids gave a strong twitch every now and then. He felt like twitching himself, and resisted popping another of the stimulant pills he'd been using to stay awake. At least Tarragon was sleeping now in his quarters.

"This being clearly comes from some other extra-dimensional planet," Marceau said. "But the woman says she's from Earth!"

"Not our Earth," said Dr. Mann. "*Another* Earth. Do you see how remarkable this is, Dr. Marceau? This development is even more exciting, more significant, than the research we were sent here to perform!"

"I understand the significance," she said, faltering, "but...but..."

Tamati stepped closer to the examination table. "What if more alternates are already here at the base, or outside right now dying in the cold? Or...what if others are on the way, but they just haven't *caught up* yet?"

The others all looked at him.

"How could that be," Marceau asked, "with the whole lab in ruins except for the pod?"

"Maybe its existence alone is enough to, I dunno, attract them," said Tamati.

"Attracting them through what physical process? Unless in these alternate realities, scientists are conducting research of the same type, sending these people out there...but we're receiving them instead."

"It seems to me," Fuseli said, "that rather than being involved in experiments on their end, these individuals are being transmitted here simply because of their relationship to Nguyen, by being iterations of the same person."

"It could be that's what's happening, but there's definitely no 'simply' about it!"

"All I know is, the woman seems genuinely unaware of how she came to be here. You think she's hiding information about some experiment on her alternate Earth? And this man here...was he some kind of terrorist, or was he just scared out of his mind by circumstances he couldn't comprehend?"

Shaking her overloaded head, Marceau looked to the Liaison. "The woman arrived immediately after Nguyen returned, but how could this man arrive here not only in a different part of the base, but days after those two appeared?"

"I cannot understand this myself, Dr. Marceau, except to say there are anomalous conditions at work. If I might venture a strong possibility, however, it would be to suggest that the accident involving our teleportation experiments opened a rift that communicates with parallel universes. And that this rift might remain open."

"Amazing," Mann said, beaming down at the corpse as if he were speaking to it directly. "Absolutely amazing."

-8-

Though reluctant to remove himself from ongoing activities for any amount of time, Fuseli went to his quarters and slept for four hours. When he emerged he paused to glance at the closed door of Rhan Luyen's room, but kept walking. He used the barracks' showers, dressed in fresh camos, and found his way to the cafeteria after asking a passing technician for directions.

As he was going in, he met Tarragon—well rested and well fed—coming out, and they stopped to talk.

"Tamati caught me up on what was said at the post mortem," Tarragon told Fuseli. He didn't look fazed by what he'd learned; just another matter to be dealt with. "He's got his people combing the base for other intruders, or whatever you'd call them. Me, I'm going with a team to drive around the outside in a rover, to see if any of these alternates have materialized out there. Not that any of them would survive for long."

"Who knows what environments they might come from, after seeing that blue-skinned guy," Fuseli said. "I'm going to catch something to eat, then I want Marceau to show me what's left inside the dome. Including that teleportation pod."

They parted ways, and Fuseli went to the cafeteria line. He saw workers of various types queued up for homegrown salad sprinkled with flavored crickets, but he opted for a cinnamon-flavored mock oatmeal made from fermented bacteria. He placed this and a black coffee on his tray, turned to look for a table where he could sit alone, but a yellow set of scrubs caught his eye. It was Rhan Luyen, sitting at a table picking at a salad while the female Colonial Forces guard who sat opposite her played a game on her wrist comp. Fuseli went over to them.

"Care if I join you?"

Rhan looked up at him and said nothing. The guard shut down her game, embarrassed, and said, "Yes sir! I mean, please do, sir!"

As Fuseli sat, he told Rhan's guard. "You taking her back to her room after this?"

"Yes, sir."

"I'll take her back for you. You can leave us."

"Oh...but, sir...my orders..."

"No worries; Lieutenant Tamati is a friend of mine. Anyway..." Fuseli tapped the insignia on one of his shoulders, identifying him as a captain.

"Of course, sir!" The grunt stood up, saluted, and walked off across the cafeteria for the exit.

Fuseli sipped his coffee, switching his attention to Rhan. She was watching him silently; unnervingly. "Has anyone told you," he asked, "what our latest theory is about you?" When she shook her head, he went on, "Though we don't know all the whys and the hows yet, I think it's only fair to tell you. We believe the accident we had here with our teleportation experiments opened up an anomaly, a portal that allows this universe to communicate with others."

"So...that's why the Earth you people talk about and the one I know aren't the same."

"Exactly."

"Is there a way to get me back to mine?"

"Well," Fuseli puffed up his cheeks, "we're only just beginning to recognize the situation, let alone knowing how to make it work for us. To be honest, I think the focus is going to be on negating this anomaly."

"Which would trap me here."

"That may very well be the case, I'm afraid."

The woman stared at him intensely for a few moments without speaking, as if Fuseli himself were responsible for this situation. However, eventually she said, "Now you know I didn't come here on purpose, or to cause any trouble. So why don't you take this monitor off my ankle and let me go free like any other person in this place? And take me back to your version of Earth, at least, until you people can maybe find a way to get me to mine?"

"Give us a little more time, and I'm sure we can do all that. Well, not so sure about the last part."

Rhan muttered a swear in the language of her parents, those immigrants from the Unnamed Country. Then, her smoldering black eyes flicked up to meet Fuseli's again. "And the guy who looks like me, in that other cell. Does he come from another Earth, too?"

"No. He's from this universe. But..." Fuseli then gave her a quick version of the events in the greenhouse, and the subsequent post mortem of the mysterious alien who, in his maddened state, had killed two of the base's staff.

"So you're saying," Rhan said, her eyes gone large and looking a little maddened herself, "that blue-skinned guy...and the guy in the room near mine..."

"They're you."

Rhan just sat there for a while, staring at him.

Lieutenant Morris Tarragon rode up front with the driver, while two other Colonial Forces soldiers—one of them being Amaka Sunday—sat behind them inside a transport rover with three sets of wheels on either side. The cabin's suspension was such that it barely jostled as the vehicle rumbled along over Titania's icy surface.

The plan was to entirely circle the pentagon-shaped arrangement of interconnected structures that constituted Base Gertrude, looking for anything out of the ordinary, before moving on to check the three distant launch stations, too. Presently they rode alongside the long hydroponics greenhouse with its hemispherical roof. All the greenery showing through its transparent sides made for a stark contrast with the beyond-frigid environment they moved through.

Tarragon twisted around in his seat. "You did good taking out that shooter, Private Sunday."

"Thank you, sir, but I wish I'd done better...and taken him out *before* he killed Private Hoxha."

"None of us are prepared for what's going on here. All we can do is improvise, based on our training. Like I said...you did fine."

For his part, Tarragon regretted complaining to Fuseli about the kid, and would gladly have put up with his jibber-jabbering again just to have him back.

"Hey, hey, right there!" the driver blurted.

Tarragon swung forward again to follow the driver's pointing hand. The driver kept the rover moving, but turned it in the direction of the figure he had spotted.

"Sure enough," Tarragon muttered, wagging his head. "Sure fucking enough."

"Lieutenant Tamati was right," Amaka said, leaning forward to look between the two men seated up front. "He said it was him who suggested someone might appear outside."

Tarragon said, "Leave it to a security chief to assess where threats might come from."

"Doesn't look too threatening to me," said the driver, pulling to a stop. "No rifle this time, anyway."

Before entering the rover back at the garage, the four had already donned suits for venturing outside, in case they needed to do just that. Now, Tarragon and the two grunts fitted on their helmets as well, each with a small cylinder of compressed air plugged into its back. In addition, Amaka and the other C-Forcer had their Drangs ready, though from the looks of things no one really felt they were going to need them. While the driver remained behind at his controls, the three soldiers crowded into the airlock bulging at one side of the ungainly-looking vehicle, and then when it was safe climbed down to the surface of Titania.

"Jesus Christ," said the other Colonial Forcer, looking around him at the landscape within the vastness of the crater named Gertrude. He'd never had to step outside the base before, but then neither had the other two. "Why didn't we just send a robot...or a drone?"

"Because we aren't cowards," Tarragon growled into his helmet mic. "Stay on task." In Titania's low gravity, he half walked and half hopped toward the figure they'd found.

The individual was more or less in an upright fetal position, propped against the outer wall of a corridor that connected one end of the greenhouse with the next structure. This spot formed a recess, but not nearly enough to have provided any shelter, and any warmth given off by the outer wall's surface had been far from sufficient to keep the stranger from freezing.

Tarragon reached out to prod the body. It was like poking a statue. "Got to give him credit. Looks like he lived long enough to try to find a way inside, with no air to breathe and minus three hundred degrees. Must've been attracted by the greenhouse windows."

The corpse was facing away from them, so Tarragon gestured for Amaka to help him turn it around for a better look. More than that, they would need to carry the body into the rover, so it could be examined by Fuseli and Dr. Mann inside.

Handing off her Drang to the other soldier, Amaka knelt down beside the frozen body and helped Tarragon handle it. Both of them had visions of the body's eyes suddenly flying open, its mouth stretching wide to emit one last dying shriek as it grabbed onto their arms with cold-hardened, claw-like fingers.

The individual was beyond dead, however...and yet, when they had moved it sufficiently to view its face they both let go of it and jolted back in surprise. "Oh my God!" Amaka cried.

Due to its huddled position, and the baggy clothing it had worn in life, they hadn't noticed until then that the figure wasn't that of a human. The face, framed in a hood it had pulled up over the back of its head, brought the truth home. There were four sucker-like orifices arranged in a circle, alternating with four lidless eyes like pale blue marbles, pressed into the grayish flesh between the orifices. In the center of this arrangement was a circular patch of many short tentacles, which must have been moist because they were crusted with ice.

"You ever seen a thing like that, Lieutenant?" asked the male grunt.

"I haven't. All right, we need to bag this ugly up before we bring it in. Who knows what virus or contamination it might be carrying."

"Is this really another version of that prisoner Nguyen?" Amaka said, still staring at what passed for the corpse's face. "At this point, maybe anybody out there in any dimension that's teleporting from one place to another is going to get sucked here by that anomaly, or whatever it is."

"Right now, who can say?"

"And just how many are going to come here, anyway?" asked the grunt holding the two Drangs.

Tarragon looked back at him, silent for a moment.

-9-

Assuring Fuseli that conditions within were no longer considered potentially hazardous, Dr. Marceau led him into the dome in which the teleportation trials had taken place...and in which had occurred the accident that had claimed the lives of almost a quarter of the base's occupants, before the arrival of those aboard the Khopesh.

The project's chief engineer, Santosh Chawla, was already inside waiting for them, but Fuseli only returned his greeting with a grunt, too distracted by what he saw all around him. The dome itself was a windowless construction, the dark material it consisted of having been 3D printed from the moon's own minerals.

All along the dome's inner circumference had been arranged a great deal of equipment, from power sources to monitoring stations right on down to workbenches and racks for supplies. Most of the technology appeared to be of Earth Colonies origin, though certain units had a different kind of look that indicated to Fuseli they'd been contributed and integrated by the Coleopteroids. Heavy cables snaked across the floor to converge at a raised platform, reached by a short series of steps. Now, much of this equipment had been blasted into shrapnel—some chunks even having embedded themselves in the inner dome, tough as it was—while for whatever reason, some of it had remained more or less intact but was blackened by fire. The stink of scorched metal and melted plastic remained strong, and Fuseli thought he could even detect the lingering stench of crisped dead bodies. He knew that smell too well from his service as a young man during the Gurm Conflict.

"Jesus," he said. "I saw some pictures, but...it really is a hell of a mess. Is any of this at all salvageable?"

"Not much, Dr. Fuseli," said Chawla. "Bits and pieces, but luckily we have our ancillary labs, where valuable data was recorded from all our experiments."

"Going from that, what do you believe happened?"

"It's pretty clear it was a power overload, which set in motion a chain reaction. But what caused the power surges we witnessed to build so quickly and overload the lab's systems, and why we couldn't contain the problem, are still matters we're trying to work out."

Fuseli took in the various techs scattered throughout the lab, some of whom had traveled here with him from Port Haven. Some teams were dismantling wreckage, others taking readings. The two typical Coleopteroids were here, too, both looking into a wall panel they had opened, a white glow from within reflecting on their black chitin. Even as it worked, the one with the perhaps faulty prosthetic limb kept twitching. Fuseli assumed the Liaison itself—who might not even possess arms inside its cloak, for all he knew—didn't actually participate in any physical work. Whatever the case, it wasn't present. Did it require rest?

"It doesn't look to me like this can be restored," Fuseli said.

"Well, it *will* be like beginning again from scratch," Chawla replied. "Bear in mind, there was nothing here when we started out...not to mention, there was no Base Gertrude at all until this project was set in motion. As dispiriting as this accident was, we can and *must* go on."

"Absolutely," said Marceau. "We can't give up on developing interplanetary teleportation, now that we know another race uses it." She lowered her voice, so those two Coleopteroids wouldn't overhear them. "I'm sure you can appreciate that, Dr. Fuseli. The Earth Colonies can't afford to be in a weaker position technologically."

Fuseli smiled. He was sure Marceau's primary concern wasn't superiority over another race, and that she was simply trying to win him over as a military man. He said, "I get it. But, right now it looks daunting, to say the least." He glanced over at the silent, enigmatic Coleopteroids, then asked Chawla in a hushed voice himself, "Have you isolated at least whether the problem originated with our contributions, or the equipment of the Bedbugs?" He winced. "Sorry... Coleopteroids."

Chawla looked to Marceau nervously, as if checking to see if she'd stop him from proceeding, but she said nothing, though her expression betrayed discomfort. Finally he said, "It would appear, right now anyway, that the issue began with the equipment of the Coleopteroids. But that's only natural, since their technology forms the foundation of this research."

"At least the pod, there, looks nice and unscathed, still," Fuseli said, indicating with a thrust of his chin the teleportation pod behind Chawla, where it rested on that scorched raised platform in the room's center. "Seeing as how it got here after the fireworks."

Whereas the tran vehicles the Coleopteroids themselves used to journey from one dimension to another put Fuseli in mind of locomotive engines of old, the prototype teleportation pod they'd helped develop for the humans made Fuseli think of a black steel bathysphere of the 1930s. But, while there was of course a hatch for the occupant to get in and out, there were no portholes or anything like a window.

Chawla walked them closer to the pod. "Aside from some calibrations being thrown off, and some bizarre readings that we're still interpreting, the pod appears to be in good shape and ready to return to work...once we have the equipment restored to send it. We could have it shipped off to Jötunn...but where would *they* teleport it to?"

"We're not shipping it off anywhere," Marceau said firmly, "nor giving it to the Coleopteroids. We need to regain the ability to launch it again, is all."

"How many passengers can this hold?" asked Fuseli.

"Only one," Chawla replied, "though of course larger shuttles would be designed, ideally."

"I can see why they said the woman couldn't have stowed away inside undetected," Fuseli noted. "It's not all that big."

"It isn't," Chawla agreed. "Let me show you the inside."

Together they mounted the steps to the platform, Fuseli and Marceau standing back to watch as Chawla accessed a program on his wrist comp that would allow him to open the heavy, riveted hatch automatically.

"Here we go," he said, tapping a button on the wrist comp's screen.

The curved hatch slid aside, and as if emerging from a gigantic egg, the creature inside the pod lunged out in a frenzy of movement. The hatchway was just wide enough for its bulk to duck through, and it thrashed its tentacle-like arms as much to free them from inside the cramped pod as to drive back the alien being the creature found itself facing when it burst free.

Marceau screamed, and Chawla might have screamed, too, if one of the creature's six upper limbs—which ended in open pincers with serrated teeth—

hadn't slashed him across the neck. With his hands flapping helplessly at his gaping, gushing throat, Chawla toppled backwards off the pod's platform.

As it pulled the rest of its body from the pod and straightened to its full height, the creature turned toward Marceau. To Fuseli, the thing resembled the Coleopteroids in general design, but whereas they were only about five feet in height, this being was well over six feet...and whereas the exoskeletons of the Coleopteroids were black, this creature's chitin was uniformly of an ivory hue. Also, it had had none of its three pairs of upper limbs removed and replaced with useful prosthetics.

Before Marceau could throw herself off the platform to escape it, and before the creature could swat her out of its way, Fuseli had already pulled his sidearm and extended it in both hands. He fired shot after shot.

He saw chunks of its armored exoskeleton fly from its head like shards of pottery, but the creature didn't go down. At least it turned its attention away from Marceau, swinging around to face Fuseli instead. He backed off from it quickly along the platform, keeping the curve of the teleportation pod partly between them. This gave Marceau the chance to jump down off the platform and run for the dome's primary exit.

The insect-like creature kept coming at Fuseli, whipping its tentacular upper limbs, each set of pincers spread open wide and seeking to tear into him. Some of the claws struck violently against the outside of the pod in their crazed lashing.

Fuseli kept on firing, now concentrating the Scythe's shots on the thing's egg-like ivory eyes.

Finally: one of the eyes cracked open, and the next bullet after that burst it into fragments, and the next shot after that plunged into the opening he had made. Though the creature was soundless, Fuseli could almost hear its agony shrieking in his mind. It fell sideways against the pod, then seemed to rebound off and it pitched from the platform to the floor. All the while, its limbs kept whipping, the pincers rattling across the floor, sounding like gunshots themselves.

Almost calmly, Fuseli jumped down from the platform himself, got closer to the creature while still keeping clear of its arms, and fired a few more shots through its ruptured eye.

Abruptly, all the limbs gave a last shudder, like the tails of rattlesnakes, and then the tentacles flopped to the floor lifelessly. From the shattered eye, a viscous translucent jelly oozed out.

Fuseli rushed to the side of Dr. Chawla and knelt over him. He was going to shout for one of the terrified technicians to bring him some sealant used in their work, so he could close the engineer's throat wound until they could get him to the med unit, but he saw it was too late. The wound had been more severe than he'd feared, and Chawla already lay dead in a pond of blood, staring at the dome's ceiling.

Fuseli looked over his shoulder at the dead alien bitterly, then snapped an order to the technicians standing around.

"Seal that pod up again—and somebody call Lieutenant Tamati. I want two guards, at *least*, to stand watch over it at all times. No one is to open it again... for *any* reason."

-10-

They were back in the med unit, and now the limited number of cryogenic chambers were starting to fill up. The one containing the body of Santosh Chawla was closed, but those containing the corpses of the alien Tarragon's team had found and the one Fuseli had killed were extended from the wall, though their transparent covers were in place in case the bodies posed any hazards that scans hadn't picked up on.

The Liaison had floated close to the chambers in that eerie way it moved, and stared down at one body and then the other.

"So," Fuseli asked, "do you recognize either type of being? How about that one there, with a face like a tapeworm?" He gestured toward the alien discovered outside. Upon further inspection—and no longer frozen in a fetal position—it had been found to possess one pair of arms, one pair of legs, and an intermediary pair of limbs that suggested they might be used as either arms or legs as needed.

"I believe this is a member of an extra-dimensional race I am familiar with," the Liaison said. "But my people have chosen not to interact with them, and do not visit their world."

"Why is that?" Marceau asked. She had put on a heavy sweater and was drinking a cup of tea, as if she needed their psychological comfort more so than their warmth to recover from what she had been through.

"We have found them to be a violent people, frequently in conflict with their own nations, which are essentially countless small armies commanded by warlords."

Tarragon was handling an odd handgun that had been found in a holster under the frozen being's garments. "I'm starting me a collection," he muttered.

"And the one that looks like it's related to your own kind?" Fuseli asked.

"A curious being," said the Liaison. "We do not have a race of this type on our home world. However, it does bear similarity to an ancestor of ours from the fossil record."

"Is this anomaly pulling people out of different time periods now, too?" Tarragon asked.

"I do not believe that to be the case, Lieutenant Tarragon," said the Liaison.

"The woman, Rhan Luyen," Fuseli said. "She says she comes from the year 2023. That doesn't mean she comes from *our* 2023, though. It just means that's the year in her alternate Earth. It could be like that with this being. It's an alternate version of you Coleopteroids, from a universe where it's still that ancient age... unless, this race in its reality never evolved into your current race."

"This is indeed a fascinating case," the Liaison said, "and demands further study by my people."

"Why are these aliens so bent on killing us when they get here, though?" Tarragon asked.

"Well," Dr. Mann spoke up, "so far they've all apparently come from less technologically advanced societies. They don't understand how they came to be here and it overwhelms them. They panic...lash out. Imagine being this pseudo Coleopteroid, for example, materializing inside that tight little pod, thinking it was imprisoned—then suddenly freed and being faced with a race it had never encountered before."

"But there is a kind of similarity between them," Fuseli observed. "Remember, our original—Tony Nguyen—is a pirate. I'll bet he's either killed a person or two in his career, or at least he's partnered with killers. Then that blue-skinned shooter...and this war-like being with the tapeworm face...and the bastard that killed Chawla..."

"And the woman?" Mann said. Fuseli didn't say anything to that, only looked over at him, so Mann continued with a little chuckle. "These beings vary so wildly in their physical makeup, but you're trying to suggest they might all share a similar personality?"

"I'm a man of science like yourself, in case you'd forgotten," Fuseli said. "I'm not suggesting they all share a common soul, and that soul is sinful...but..."

"But?"

Again, Fuseli didn't respond.

Mann's smile widened. "But you are sort of thinking that, aren't you?"

"Not about sinful," Fuseli finally said. "I don't think in those terms. But if they *are* alternate versions of the same self, I don't know why they shouldn't bear some resemblance in terms of personality traits. Shaped, of course, by their individual circumstances...their cultures, religions, political situations..."

"In any case," Mann said, stepping closer to stare down at the body of the beetle-like alien in its cryo drawer, "if any more of them appear here, we must try to capture them alive."

"To start a menagerie?" Fuseli said.

"To study them! Interview them...learn from them. Even with the teleportation project ruined, this base has still become an entryway for beings we've never encountered before. That even the Coleopteroids have never encountered before! The studies we can conduct here are of immeasurable value. I'm sure if we can only try harder to capture any further beings alive, using nonlethal methods instead of bullets, we can calm these beings down...reason with them. Just as we've done with the woman."

"I'd be happy to spare their lives," Fuseli said, "if they'd only give us the chance to do so. But I'm sure Dr. Marceau, for one, is grateful for how things turned out in her own encounter."

"Just think if we could isolate this rift," Mann said, "and learn how to utilize it deliberately. It could open up explorations and travel far beyond even what your people—" he nodded at the Liaison "—are presently capable of."

"That could very well be a possibility my superiors will discuss as further information is gathered. It is fortunate that a new team of my people will be shipped here as soon as they teleport to our station on Earth."

"How about Jötunn?" Fuseli asked Marceau. "Still nothing unusual being seen there?"

"Nothing out of the ordinary on their end," she replied.

"And if more visitors just keep popping up?" Tarragon said.

"We'll have to build onto the base to accommodate them," said Mann.

"I'm talking...what if they just don't stop coming here? There are infinite parallel universes, aren't there? I'm saying, what if millions...*billions* of beings pour through here?"

"I hardly think—"

"Why couldn't that happen?" Fuseli said.

"Well..." Mann trailed off.

"We should really isolate that rift, if it can be isolated, and confine it if it can be confined."

"I hope you're not suggesting we try to reverse it or close it up."

"If we can, maybe we should."

"Did you not hear what I said, about the possibilities it presents?" Mann blurted.

"And did you not hear what Lieutenant Tarragon said, about the threat it presents?"

"All this means," Marceau cut in, "is that we need to know more. Investigate further."

"And stay on guard," said Tarragon.

Fuseli sighed. He felt in over his head. He'd only come here to help understand the situation with that one mysterious woman...

He said, "I need to report to General Stroud. I've got a lot to fill him in on. This is bigger than any of us signed up for. Personally, until we get a better idea of what's happening and for how long it's going to happen, I'd prefer to see this entire base evacuated for safety's sake."

"Now Doctor," Marceau said, "that isn't your call to make."

"Of course it isn't, but it could be my recommendation."

"And what then, if more visitors arrive and there's no one here to see to them?" Mann demanded, growing openly angry. "We leave them to their own devices? To starve, or fight amongst themselves? Perhaps you're suggesting on our way out we throw all the hatches open, let the air out and the cold in, so the visitors will die out as soon as they arrive. A simple solution!"

"I'm not saying we turn our backs on the problem and leave that rift to just continue doing what it's doing...but I'm thinking of the safety of our people here, first and foremost."

"Ah yes, just as you thought of the safety of your relief ship's crew on the planet W-18, and abandoned the indigenous people you had gone there to assist. Leaving them to starve."

"If you know anything about that situation," Fuseli said, his gaze on Mann akin to a laser beam boring into the man, "then you're well aware that those beings were attacking us...killing us, in order to *eat* us."

"Dr. Mann," Marceau said, putting a hand on his arm, but the medical chief had already been convinced to drop the matter by Fuseli's menacing glare.

"As I said," Fuseli went on, in an even tone that somehow sounded more deadly than if he had shouted in rage, "I've got a call to my boss to make." And with that, he nodded at Tarragon and the two of them left the med unit together, Tarragon tucking the alien handgun into a pocket of his camos.

-11-

To conserve space, most of the tiny individual rooms that made up the barracks featured bunk beds, and thus accommodated two people each. Except in a few cases involving married couples, men and women generally didn't room together. Though it was discouraged, however, it was inevitable that some of the personnel would become romantically—or at least sexually—involved during their assignment at Base Gertrude, regardless of their relationship status back home, wherever home was for them. These relationships might involve one's roommate (the most convenient arrangement) or someone else of the same sex, but any combination was possible. Accommodating roommates would often make themselves scarce for a few hours so a lover might come to visit the other.

Amelie Brun was one of the power plant's operators, and her roomie Eesha had obligingly gone out to jog a few circuits through the base's connecting buildings to give Ame some privacy while her latest entanglement, Oskar Karlsson, slipped in for a visit. With her long blond-dyed hair, smoky eyes and equally smoky British accent, and a seductive smile of beguilingly crooked teeth, Ame had had more than one entanglement since taking the assignment at Base Gertrude.

Good-looking and naturally blond Kar was one of the techs in charge of maintaining the base's robots and certain other automated processes. He was a more recent arrival than Ame, and they had caught each other's eye immediately. When he arrived at Ame's room, she was already down to a too-small undershirt and panties, and within seconds she had his shirt over his head and tossed to the floor.

"Pretty boy," she purred, running her hands over his smooth, hairless chest before lunging in to suckle at one pink nipple. Kar laughed nervously and squirmed a little at the force with which she sucked, and flinched when she bit down a little, but he held her head there. While Ame seemingly nursed, they both sank down to the lower bunk. Eesha had politely agreed to take the upper bunk, being smaller in stature anyway.

On the bed, Ame worked at opening Kar's trousers while switching from suckling his nipple to sucking hard at the surrounding flesh of his breast. She often took pleasure in leaving the dark bruises of hickeys against his contrasting paleness. "Just marking my territory," she said, coming up for air. "Mm, you smell nice and manly today."

"So do you," he said.

She grabbed him by the throat and forced him onto his back. "Oh, I do, do I?" She reached behind her to yank his shoes off and toss them across the room, so as to next pull his trousers down his legs roughly.

As Ame was applying her mouth in another way, with Kar holding her head again and watching her in a kind of stunned bliss, an odd sound managed to intrude into his awareness. It was something like a jabbering human voice, squeaky and badly distorted, mixed with the chittering of an angry squirrel. He glanced over toward the room's flip-down desk and its accompanying chair. What he saw there, crouched as if to hide in the inadequate shadow under the desk, caused him to sit up sharply.

"What?" Ame said, looking up at Kar and seeing how he stared across the room. Had Eesha returned too early?

The creature was about a foot and a half tall standing on its hind legs, its clawed forelegs held close to its front in fear. It wore no clothing, so it was plain to see how its translucent pink flesh—marbled purple and blue beneath—hung from its body in baggy wrinkles upon wrinkles. It was hairless except for white bristles sprouting from head and body at random, and its face was vaguely like a human skull covered loosely in that thin, wrinkly skin. In its deep skull sockets, the creature's bead-like red eyes were barely perceptible—protected as they were behind the outermost layer of skin—but its teeth were only too distinct: a massive pair of curved, rodent-like incisors, matched by another pair below. Other than that its mouth appeared toothless, a puckered black hole that emitted the strange sounds Kar had been hearing.

"Look!" he said, pushing at Ame's shoulders to get her off him. "What is that thing?"

"What thing?" Ame looked where he was gawking, and when she spotted the creature she cried out, aghast. "Oh my God...don't let it near me! You have to catch it!"

"Did it escape from one of the labs?" Kar babbled, swinging his legs over the side of the bed. "A monkey, or..."

"There are no test animals here!" Ame pulled the pillowcase off her pillow and passed it to him. "Catch it in this! We have to show security!"

"*Me* catch it?" Kar said, but he held the pillowcase open. "Can't we wait for security?"

Ame looked around for where she'd set aside her wrist comp, and spotted it atop the desk. There was no way she could bring herself to go near the creature to retrieve it.

Naked, his arousal starting to subside but his exposed member still pointing the way forward, Kat advanced on the creature one timid step. "Hey...come here. I won't hurt you..."

The creature's bizarre vocalizations grew louder and more agitated, and it backed itself against the wall. It had nowhere else to go. With the door to the room closed, Kar couldn't understand how it had even come to be here. Small as it was, it still couldn't have come through the room's narrow, securely covered ventilation grille.

"Come on, come on," Kar said in the same gentle tone he used with his mother's cats back in the Mars colony where his parents lived. This couldn't be any worse than getting a pill into one of them. He cursed the desk for being in his way; otherwise he thought he might have easily lunged forward and got the pillowcase over it before it could dart to either side.

The creature didn't dart to either side. Instead, as Kar took one more wary step forward, cooing to the thing, it sprang into the air straight at him...and latched itself onto his face.

Ame's scream rivaled Kar's own. She watched in a paralysis of terror as Kar spun away from the desk, grabbing at the thing that had seized onto his head in a frantic effort to wrench it away. Meanwhile, the creature was ripping at one of his ears with its incisors.

Ame finally scrambled off the bed, picked up the chair that went with the flip-down desk, reversed it in her hands, and stabbed at the creature with one of the chair's legs. The way Kar was staggering about wildly, though, trying to get a grip on the thing's maniacally clawing limbs, she ended up striking him more times than she did the creature. All she really accomplished was to cause it to switch from tearing up Kar's ear to focusing its attack on his nose instead.

Ame dropped the chair, snatched her wrist comp off the desk, and clasped it on her arm. She punched in the emergency code, and immediately shouted her room number to the security officer who answered.

In his desperate dance around the room, Kar finally spun into a wall, bounced off, and crashed to the floor. His sobs and screams were muffled by the pressure of the creature's body against the front of his face. He rolled back and forth on the floor, his heels drumming helplessly.

Ame looked around her, spotted her handbag on a shelf, snatched it up and dug around inside. She pulled forth a steel nail file with a pointed tip at one end. Gripping this in her fist, she rushed to Kar's side, knelt down on the floor beside him, and drew her arm back to stab downward at the creature's back. She was afraid Kar's crazed movements would cause her to miss and strike him instead, maybe even a killing blow to his carotid artery, but the tip of the file plunged into the thing's horribly wrinkled body. It shrieked, but its teeth were so deep into Kar's face that it didn't let go, so she stabbed it again...again...

Her door buzzed. Over its speaker someone called, "Security!"

Leaving the blood-slicked file stuck in the creature's back, Ame jumped to her feet, rushed to the door and unlocked it. Instantly, Rhys Tamati and another member of security pushed past her naked, blood-spattered body, Tamati with handgun drawn and the grunt with a Drang gripped in his fists. When Tamati saw the thing attached to Kar's face, however, he barred the grunt with his arm to keep him from overreacting. Then, Tamati got down beside Kar, pressed his handgun against the creature at a sideways angle so he wouldn't send a bullet through its body and into Kar's face—and fired.

Much of the creature's guts were blown out the far side of its body and it instantly went limp, though its double sets of incisors were still lodged in Kar's face. Through all the blood, Tamati couldn't as yet gauge the severity of his wounds, but they didn't appear life-threatening...unless the thing had just transferred some deadly alien bacteria they weren't in a position to deal with. Tamati put his hands around the thing to test whether he might remove it himself, but thought better of it. All he accomplished was to cause one of Kar's eyes to slide out from under the dead creature, dislodged as it was from its socket but hanging on by a scrap.

Kar was only whimpering now, close to losing consciousness from blood loss and shock. Resting a hand on the man's chest to reassure him, Tamati twisted around to order his grunt to call the med unit, but he saw Ame was already on her wrist comp and doing just that through her sobbing gasps.

When she was finished, she looked up at Tamati and asked, "Is Kar dead?"

Tamati shifted his body a little to block her from seeing the young man's head. "No. Where did that thing come from?"

"I don't *know!*" she cried. "We saw it hiding under my desk, there! Do you know what it is?"

"Yes," Tamati said grimly. "I do."

-12-

Dr. Marceau entered the medical unit just after Fuseli had finished working on the still unconscious maintenance tech, Oskar Karlsson. Dr. Mann, who had assisted Fuseli with the surgical procedures, looked up smiling at the project leader as she came toward the operating table, but she didn't step within its brightly-lit aseptic field.

"Well?" Through the field she looked down at the young man, but he was still under anesthesia and wore what looked like a full-head mask of black plastic vacuum-formed to his face, with openings for his nostrils and mouth. In addition, air was being fed into him via a nasal cannula.

"Dr. Fuseli did an admirable job," said Mann. "He's as much a cosmetic surgeon as a trauma surgeon."

"I'd have done a lot better if I had him at our facility at Port Haven," Fuseli said. "The equipment here is pretty basic, but that's to be expected. I do hope I can take him back to Port Haven with me when this is all sorted, so I can polish things up right. I can have him looking prettier than he did before the attack."

"Is it safe to keep him here, or should he be moved from Base Gertrude now?" Marceau asked.

"He'll be okay recovering here," Fuseli said, looking more severely at Marceau across Kar's prone body, "but I'm thinking it would actually be better for *all* of us to be moved from Base Gertrude."

"Doctor, we've been through this. You spoke to your commanding officer, didn't you? What did he have to say?"

Fuseli sighed, dropping his gaze back to Kar. "General Stroud told me it may come to the point where there's unequivocally no choice but to evacuate the base, but at this time his superiors want us to remain here to observe, record, report."

"You see? This is an unprecedented situation. If any anomalous scientific phenomenon warrants study, it's this!"

"I do understand a lot can be learned from studying all this," Fuseli said. "But you can see that things are only getting more dangerous here."

"I spoke to my superiors, too," said Marceau. "Rather than pull us out, they feel the response should be to send in a good many *more* scientists, technicians, and the security to protect them. It's just a matter of assembling the team, getting them out here to Titania, and finding a way to accommodate them when we're already limited for space."

Dr. Mann offered, "We could simply work different shifts and rotate rest time in the barracks...and we could also perhaps allow personnel to bunk in our ships, even the trams and tram hub, until we can create some new habitat modules."

"Yes," Marceau said, "we can and will find a way. It's only a matter of logistics."

"That's all it is?" Fuseli said, waving his hand at Kar. "Tell that to this guy."

Standing toward the back of the operating room, beside a robot that had assisted but now stood in sleep mode, Rhys Tamati spoke up. "How big or small can these alternates get? This one was pretty small, and it didn't seem all that advanced. More like an animal. Could we find ourselves dealing with a whole plague of alien microorganisms that correspond with Tony Nguyen?"

Dr. Mann laughed. "Oh, Lieutenant! This latest specimen that you largely destroyed may not have been as advanced as a human—and I say maybe, because we can't be certain—but it was surely still a sentient being. I can't imagine any alternate version of Mr. Nguyen would be anything but."

"But you can't say for certain," Tamati insisted, stepping closer to the glow of the aseptic field. "We're in totally unknown waters here, and I'm not liking it."

"Your displeasure is duly noted, Lieutenant," Mann said, turning away from him.

They all moved back from the operating table as a nurse and another robot came forward to enter the field, set the table to mobile mode, then wheel it away to a nice quiet recovery room where Kar could be monitored. Sullenly, Tamati watched them go. He asked, "And you scanned him for alien bacteria and viruses?"

"What do you think, Lieutenant?"

"And what if they were so alien the scans wouldn't be able to detect them?"

Mann only chuckled and wagged his head. Tamati didn't care for this response, and took two ominous steps toward the medical chief before Fuseli held out a palm to warn him back. Fuseli said, "You did good saving this man, Lieutenant. Glad you got there so quick. Now, why don't you go take a rest for a couple-three hours?"

"Sir, there could be more and more of these things pouring into every part of this base even as we *speak!*" Tamati said. "How am I supposed to rest?"

"You won't be any good if you don't. I'm ordering you...go to your quarters. I've got Lieutenant Tarragon on patrol, and your own people are on the case, too."

Tamati exhaled slowly, nodded, saluted Fuseli. "Yes, sir." He turned and walked crisply toward the operating room's exit.

When the security chief had gone, Mann commented, "Well, that was somewhat scary."

"You're going to see more and more people on edge," Fuseli said. "Get used to it. And you should hold a personnel meeting, or make an intercom announcement. Let everyone know exactly what the situation is here, with these alternate beings."

"Logistically speaking," Marceau said, "since the meeting room is too small and not even the cafeteria could accommodate everyone, I think a remote meeting over our wrist comps is best."

"I'd get on that, then," Fuseli said. "Of course, even armed with the full story, how well can people protect themselves when these beings can teleport right into your locked room?"

"I'm curious why none of them, yet, have been teleported half inside a wall," Mann said. "Or fused with one of us who got in the way."

"I imagine," Fuseli said, "the Bedbugs could explain. Their technology must prohibit accidents like that, somehow. But if only it could have prohibited the rest of what's happened."

"I still contend," Mann said, "that this development is a boon, not a tragedy. Well, I mean...aside from the deaths involved."

"Of course," Fuseli said. "Aside from that little detail."

-13-

With Chief Engineer Santosh Chawla dead, the investigation of the cause for the teleportation mishap had been assumed by several of the technicians that had come to Base Gertrude with Fuseli on the Khopesh. Restlessly, he had returned to the dome to see if anyone was any closer to an answer for what had happened, and was happening.

He was satisfied to see two security people armed with Drang assault engines posted inside the dome, as he had ordered. Looking past them, he saw one of the new technicians standing outside the bathysphere-like teleportation pod, taking readings beside a mobile cart bearing equipment that was plugged into a port on the pod's exterior. Fuseli went over to speak with this Asian woman, whose name eluded him. She looked up at his approach and nodded in greeting.

Fuseli glanced up at the pod, frowning. "Shouldn't we power this thing down completely until we have some answers? I'm afraid more unwanted guests are going to pop up inside it."

"Captain Fuseli, we won't *have* any answers unless we keep it powered up to run diagnostics. Don't worry, it's been kept sealed per your order. Anyway, we have a camera inside...there's been one all along. Chief Engineer Chawla got careless opening the pod without checking the camera feed first."

"So no one has seen anything else appear in there?"

"Not since the thing that killed Mr. Chawla."

"Listen," Fuseli said, looking around to see if the Coleopteroids were present within the dome. Apparently not. He assumed they had retired to their own living space, in a dedicated building beyond the regular barracks. It had to be pretty empty in there, these days. "The Coleopteroid Liaison made a comment, when I first met it, that it thought they were getting close to an answer about what happened."

"I've heard the Liaison make a comment like that, too," the tech said.

"But did it say what it thought that answer might be?"

"No, Captain."

"Why wouldn't it share its suspicions with you, since they're supposed to be working in conjunction with our team?"

"No idea. Maybe they don't want to influence us as we try to draw our own conclusions. They might not have enough evidence yet to back up whatever their suspicions are."

Fuseli grunted, unsatisfied with these possibilities, as he scowled again at the black sphere—sitting there on its pedestal like some sinister alien idol.

His wrist comp beeped. He excused himself and stepped away from the tech to take the call, and found himself looking at Tarragon on his device's small screen.

"We seem to have had a sighting of another alternate," Tarragon reported. "A mechanic for the ground vehicles said he saw it looking into the garage through a window. When the guy yelled, it acted startled like it could hear him and ran off."

"Ran off? Out there, in that cold, without any kind of breathable atmosphere?"

"Apparently. The mechanic is credible. He described the thing as big...*really* big. Maybe twenty feet tall. He said it looked like it was bending down to peek inside. Said it looked like a giant crab, maybe, but all covered in gray fur."

"Jesus. So where are you now? Looks like you're outside, too."

"I ran down to the garage as soon as I heard and grabbed the rover again, but we haven't found any trace of the thing yet. Maybe it's fast, or there's a cave nearby or something. We'll keep looking."

"Well, don't stray too far from the base. I'm sure Tamati's people have drones. Get them to send some of those up to look for it."

"Okay, I'll do that. We're just going to go out a little further to a rock formation up ahead, then we'll swing back in."

"Man oh man, Morris."

"What are you up to now?" Tarragon asked.

"Guess I'm going to go meet up with Marceau and Mann again," Fuseli said. "Now that we know that woman Rhan Luyen is an alternate, they said they want to interview her some more, try to learn a bit about this parallel Earth she says she's from."

"Parallel Earth," Tarragon echoed. "We sure did walk into something here, didn't we?"

"Sure did," said Fuseli.

Fuseli cut the call and started for the dome's exit, but heard his name called and looked around to see the tech he'd been speaking with hurry toward him. When she reached him to speak, she kept her voice low.

"Captain, it might be premature or even irresponsible for me to say this... especially since we can't be sure, with so much equipment having been destroyed in the explosion, but...ah..."

"Yes?"

"Well," she went on hesitantly, leading Fuseli to think she'd been too reluctant before to say whatever she had to say, "based on my own examinations so far, and comparing notes with survivors of the original team...uh, what I mean to say is, it doesn't appear to me that the cause of the problem was our own technology."

"Don't worry, Chawla shared that same sentiment with me already. But you're saying you've come to the same conclusion...that it was likely their equipment. The Bedbugs."

"The what? Oh, yes...the Coleopteroids. Again, to be fair, their technology and ours was so integrated that it's hard to isolate something like that. *However...*"

"However, at present that's your assessment. That whatever went wrong, it was on their end."

"Yes sir," the tech said in her confidential tone. "That's what it's looking like to me."

-14-

When Fuseli met with Dr. Marceau and Dr. Mann in the cafeteria, where they had said they were going to bring Rhan Luyen for their interview, he was surprised to see Anthony Nguyen seated at the same long table with them. Marceau sat beside Nguyen on one side, with Mann and Rhan facing them on the other side. At the far end of the table, keeping an eye on the proceedings, were two security grunts—both making a good show of glowering threateningly.

"Here comes Captain Whoever now," Rhan Luyen remarked, smiling like a cat as she watched Fuseli approach the table.

Rather than sit just yet, Fuseli looked from Rhan to Nguyen and back again. Nguyen was smiling at him, too.

"I make for a beautiful woman," Nguyen said, "don't you think?"

"I do prefer you that way," Fuseli said, "I have to admit."

Nguyen snorted, and Rhan's cat smile widened subtly. Fuseli took a seat on the same side as Marceau and Nguyen. Marceau, who was recording the interview on her wrist comp, leaned around the test subject to speak with Fuseli.

"This is beyond fascinating, Dr. Fuseli. We've been having them compare details about their lives. Of course, there are major differences, besides the obvious. Anthony having been raised on Port Cygon space station, and Rhan in a small rural town, but there are also remarkable similarities. Both their mothers having five brothers. One of Anthony's uncles having been killed in a hoverbike accident at Port Cygon, and one of Rhan's uncles killed in a motorcycle accident back in that Unnamed Country she immigrated from. Similarities between the names of certain relatives..."

"We could go on with this all day," Mann said. "It truly is mind-blowing. The similarities are of course trivial individually, but taken as a whole..."

"What kind of life have you left back home, in case you can never get back there?" Fuseli asked Rhan, interrupting Mann. "Which, as I've said, is unfortunately pretty unlikely. Do you have a husband?"

"Are you asking me if I'm available?" Rhan said, those smoldering eyes of hers seeming to penetrate him slyly.

Nguyen had been about to sip from his cup of coffee but lowered it, barking a laugh. "Be careful there, Captain Fuseli...I claim this beauty for myself."

Rhan looked across at Nguyen as if he'd gone mad. "Oh really? You'd want to be with a female version of yourself?"

"Just think if we had a baby," Nguyen said. "If me and another me had a baby, would that be a *me*, too?"

"Trust me...you'll never find out," Rhan said, turning to face Fuseli again. "I'm divorced. How about you, Captain? Do you have a wife back home, wherever that is for you?"

"Nowhere really, these days, but no...I'm divorced, also."

"I see."

"Look at her—she's interested, too," Nguyen chuckled, wagging his head.

"Children back home?" Fuseli asked.

At this, Rhan's playful mood turned dark. She began playing with her own coffee cup, watching it as she turned it in circles on the tabletop as if trying to crack a safe's combination. "I have one daughter. She's fourteen...lives with her father. Let's just say, if I never see her again it will stab me in the heart every day for the rest of my life. But...it will be better for her."

"What do you mean by that?"

"Just that I haven't always made the best decisions in life. I think she must be ashamed of me."

"Why should she be? You're just a warehouse worker like you said, doing your best," Fuseli said, watching her face carefully. "Right?"

"Yeah...right."

"Have you ever been in trouble with the law?"

Rhan's eyes jumped up to meet his again. "Why do you ask me that?" she demanded.

"Why *do* you ask her that?" said Marceau.

"Well, it's what you just said, about poor life choices. Also, we were talking about similarities between you and Tony Nguyen, here. Tony was in jail, before he signed up for this project."

"Oh, I get it," Dr. Mann said. "You're on again about that theory of yours, Dr. Fuseli...one sinful soul shared by an infinite number of physical vessels."

"I'm simply curious about fascinating similarities, just like you and Dr. Marceau."

"So you think I'm evil," Rhan said, "along with this guy here, and all those monsters that have come through."

"Not *evil*," Fuseli replied. "Maybe...inclined toward questionable behavior. Hostility...even violence." He addressed Marceau. "I'd still like to run a truth scan on her."

"Look..." Marceau began.

Rhan snapped, "I wouldn't consent to something like that! You can imagine anything you want about me!"

Nguyen said, "Looks like you're not getting laid after all, Captain. You blew it."

"Dr. Fuseli," Marceau sighed, exasperated, "these two have been very cooperative and helpful. Can you please not antagonize them so we can continue with our interview?"

"Yeah, getting back to similarities," Nguyen said, "I think it's crazy that we both have almost the same birthmark on our left cheek." He tapped his own port-wine stain. "I suggest Rhan and I remove our clothes so we can look for any other distinguishing marks or scars we might share. We could do it in private, if everyone else is too embarrassed." He winked across at Rhan, as if mugging in a mirror.

"It's creepy watching you try to seduce yourself," Fuseli said. "It's like watching you masturbate."

"I bet you'd like watching me masturbate," Nguyen told him. "That is, to watch *that* me do it." He gestured toward Rhan.

"That's one big difference between the two of us right there," Rhan grumbled. "You're a disgusting pig, and I'm not." She addressed Fuseli again. "Have any of these weird alien versions of me had a birthmark like this, too? Besides that guy with blue skin?"

"Ah, no...I guess," Fuseli said. "Not that I've noticed, looking at the bodies. I mean, the other alternates have had very different physical structures from humans, of course."

Just then, he thought of something like a birthmark he *had* seen, actually, on the body of a sentient being that wasn't human. An image of that being rose up in his mind, as if a camera had suddenly zoomed in on it.

"Jesus H. Christ," he hissed.

"What is it?" Marceau asked. "Is something wrong, Doctor?"

"I want to go talk to the Liaison. It wasn't in the dome just now, so it must be in their quarters. Do you have a way to contact it, to tell it I want to meet with it as soon as possible?"

"Yes," Marceau said, "I can call their quarters." She opened a channel on her wrist comp.

"Tell the Liaison I want to speak to it *alone*," Fuseli stressed.

-15-

In an act of good faith, since Fuseli had asked for the Liaison to meet him alone, not accompanied by the two surviving technicians, he too had not brought any security members as bodyguards. He did, however, wear his sidearm in its holster, hidden under his black greatcoat. Given the secrecy the Liaison had demonstrated, he couldn't afford to trust the strange being unreservedly.

They met in the garage where the base's ground vehicles were kept and maintained. Fuseli was relieved to see that the rover Tarragon had taken out on patrol, along with a driver and a backup grunt, had returned. Beyond the row of parked vehicles was the garage's airlock, that gave access to the frozen hell beyond. Along another wall were a number of narrow horizontal windows that gave a view of the outside, and Fuseli remembered what Tarragon had told him one of the garage mechanics had witnessed.

Right now, the mechanics were relaxing in a little office area on the other side of the garage, per Fuseli's request, so he stood alone in the large open space as he watched the tall, black-robed Liaison glide in his direction like an apparition.

"Thanks for meeting me," he said, when the entity with its androgynous death mask of a face had reached him.

"I hope I can be of assistance to you, Dr. Fuseli. May I ask what it is you wished to meet with me about in this way?"

"Of course," Fuseli said. "I wanted to ask you about one of your surviving technicians...the one with the twitching prosthetic. Do you know why it has that tic?"

"I assume it is because the technician you speak of is under stress, as are we all."

If the Liaison was under stress, Fuseli couldn't detect it. "Does that tech have a name?"

"Not that I can convey to you. For the sake of convenience, you may refer to it as Technician 2. This, because it was second in rank when we still possessed our full team. Technician 1 was in the dome at the time of the accident, and was killed."

"Technician 2's tic caused me to notice it more than the other one."

"That would be Technician 8."

"I see. In any case, because Technician 2 caught my eye, I happened to notice that it has a grayish blotch, here, on the left side of its head." Fuseli tapped his own temple.

"Yes. You are observant, Doctor."

"Is it a birthmark?"

"I would imagine it is."

"Has it not struck you as odd, that Anthony Nguyen, his alternate self Rhan Luyen, and that stranger with the blue skin all have or had a blotch of roughly similar shape and size on that side of their head?"

Fuseli watched the Liaison's face for even the slightest flicker of a muscle. He was not rewarded, but he felt the long empty pause was significant. At last, the Liaison said, "What are you suggesting, Dr. Fuseli?"

"That maybe Technician 2 is yet another alternate form of Tony Nguyen. Or...vice versa."

"It is not possible, Dr. Fuseli. We Coleopteroids, as you call us, are not alternate versions of your kind, nor the other way around."

"You're extra-dimensional beings, though. From a different plane than ourselves...an alternate universe. Who's to say that we aren't different versions of each other, in a sense, and this is simply the first you yourself have become aware of it?"

"To our knowledge, in all our travels to other universes, we have never encountered beings that were alternate versions of ourselves."

"Until now, perhaps. Until whatever rift this accident tore open. Isn't it just possible?"

"With all respect, I cannot believe it, Doctor. However...I will notify my superiors of your comments."

"Please do. In the meantime...that birthmark on Technician 2's head?"

"A coincidence."

"A coincidence? Do you truly believe that?"

Another protracted pause. Then finally: "If you will excuse me, Dr. Fuseli, I believe I should relay your comments to my superiors immediately."

"You do that. And I'm sorry if I've distressed or annoyed you, but I'm simply trying to wrap my head around all this."

"As are we all. Thank you, Doctor, and if you'll excuse me."

Fuseli watched the robed entity swivel around, then float away from him toward the door through which it had entered.

-16-

Tarragon had indeed returned from his patrol of the area around Base Gertrude, and he called Fuseli from the security office, saying he'd like to give his report in person. When Fuseli got there, he found Rhys Tamati waiting for him, too, the security chief's nap over but his tense face making him look less than properly rested.

"Came back with something to show you," Tarragon said.

The two men made way for Fuseli to observe a control board, with rows of monitor screens mounted above it and a number of holographic monitors floating in the air as well. Tarragon reached over to tap one of the holographic screens to activate a video.

"We took this from the rover," he explained. "What you see that thing climbing on is the lip of the crater Gertrude. It's pretty high up...the going's too rough for us to have followed, even if you hadn't told us not to stray far from base. Once it got over the top, we couldn't see it anymore from below."

The video showed a view from the rover, down in the vast crater's basin, but the camera had zoomed in on its subject. Still, the creature had climbed up over the rim of the crater swiftly, then passing out of view on the other side as Tarragon had said, so the footage lasted only seconds.

"Your witness wasn't wrong," Fuseli said. "When I heard a giant crab with fur, I thought, okay...so a spider. But have you ever seen pictures of a Japanese spider crab? Of course, they're extinct now..."

"Look at the size of that thing," Tamati said. "Just its legs alone."

The creature the three men watched in the brief video, which played in a continuous loop, appeared to possess ten tremendously long, jointed legs in total, with the forelegs ending in smallish pincers. Though it was mostly silhouetted against the blue crescent of Uranus dominating the sky, Fuseli could make out the shagginess of the creature's outline.

"What are those tube-like things all over the back of its shell, do you think?" Tamati asked. "Giant barnacles from its world?"

"Probably some sort of organ," Fuseli said. "Maybe even something that helps it survive out in that environment."

"Even if I could have kept chasing it," Tarragon said, "then what? I mean, the rover has a mounted gun, but are we killing these things on sight now?"

"No," said Fuseli. "Like Dr. Mann says, as unlikely as it may seem, these things could all be sentient beings. We can't just kill them unless they display hostility. Though, given how freaked out they must feel to find themselves here—as Rhan Luyen put it—I can imagine hostility bred from fear would come naturally."

"I'll send out a few drones," Tamati said, "just to see if we can find it, keep track of its movements."

"Good," said Fuseli, his gaze still fixed on the looping video of the immense crab-thing scrambling up over the ridge of the crater called Gertrude.

"It's crazy that it looks so much like a crab," Tamati said.

"Not so crazy," Fuseli said. "The crab form works. Ever hear of carcinization? Convergent evolution? Nature loves a crab."

"Are these things getting less and less human every time?" Tarragon said. "Are they, like, coming from farther and farther away dimensions?"

"Damned if I know," said Fuseli.

Abruptly, an alert beeped not only on the wrist comps of all three men, but came over the security office's speakers as well...followed by an agitated voice.

"Emergency!" cried the voice. Fuseli recognized it as that of Private Amaka Sunday. "There's been an attack outside the Coleopteroids' living quarters! One soldier down! Attacker has a firearm!"

"Fuck," Tamati said, snatching a Drang assault engine out of a wall rack.

Fuseli and Tarragon exchanged a look, then both of them grabbed a Drang and powered it up, as well.

Tamati kept a running exchange with his security people as they raced toward their destination: the corridor between the human staff's barracks and the living quarters of the Coleopteroid team. He was told his people on scene had already called for the med unit to come take away the wounded Colonial Forcer, but when they arrived at the corridor the two medical responders were just getting the man onto a stretcher, while a dog-like med robot stood nearby.

Fuseli went straight to the injured man, while Tarragon and Tamati took positions outside the door to the Coleopteroids' quarters. There, Amaka and three other security members covered the entrance, with more Colonial Forcers coming running from both ends of the corridor, some armored up and with Drangs, but others simply in camos and gripping handguns. Standing out among those clustered near the quarters' open doorway was the Liaison. All of these people kept back to either side of the doorway, out of sight of the shooter inside.

Fuseli saw that the wounded soldier had apparently lost his entire bottom jaw. The man's eyes sought Fuseli's miserably, as he made muffled sounds behind the emergency seal the medics had used to cover the severe wound. A breathing tube ran through the seal.

"You'll be okay, soldier," Fuseli assured him, hand on his arm. "I'll make you like new myself...I promise."

He watched as the stretcher was lifted onto the quadruped robot's back and secured, and the man was borne away toward the med unit. Then, he turned to approach Amaka, who was crouched near the edge of the doorway, Drang held ready.

"What happened?" he asked, quietly to avoid being overheard in the large single room that made up the Coleopteroids' quarters. "The shooter is a Bedbug, isn't it?"

"Yes, sir," Amaka replied, still breathless from what she'd gone through. "It has Private Townsend's gun. A couple people walking to the barracks heard a commotion going on in the Coleopteroids' quarters, so they came and got us. When Private Townsend and I were almost to the door, all of a sudden it opened and one of the Coleopteroids jumped out. Townsend was startled so he brought up his gun, but the Coleopteroid grabbed his face with one of those machine arms it has...and it tore his jaw right off. It all happened so *fast!* With its other arms, it got Townsend's Drang away from him. I raised my weapon to fire, but I was afraid to hit Townsend...he was standing between us! Then, the Coleopteroid ducked back into their quarters. I started to go after it, but it fired at me and I had to take cover out here."

Fuseli put a hand on her armored shoulder to calm her. "Were you hit?"

"Only here." She motioned with her chin toward two indentations in her chest armor. "Lucky I was fully suited up for my patrol."

"Good." Fuseli looked over to see the Liaison watching him, and for the first time realized the unearthly being had been injured as well. He hurried to its side.

Closer to it, Fuseli saw a neat, bloodless opening in one of the Liaison's cheeks, like a hole punched into a Halloween mask. On that side, too, the top of the ear had been sheared off. Again, no blood came from the wound, and yet the torn flesh didn't look synthetic to Fuseli.

"You're injured," he said. "You should go to the med unit, too."

"That won't be necessary, Dr. Fuseli."

"It's Technician 2, isn't it? You brought up what we talked about."

"Yes. Technician 2 became very agitated with me about the subject. When Technician 8 tried to intervene, Technician 2 attacked us."

"Where is Technician 8 now?" Fuseli asked, looking around. Now there were four security members grouped at either side of the door, with Tarragon and Tamati on this side, as well. No sign of the other Coleopteroid.

"Technician 8 is dead," the Liaison stated. "When Technician 8 tried to subdue Technician 2, Technician 2 sought to flee from our quarters...but was met by two security people in this hallway. Technician 2 attacked one of the security people and seized his weapon, then retreated into our quarters again. Technician 2 fired at the other security person to drive her back, but when Technician 8 attempted to get the weapon away, Technician 2 fired again and killed Technician 8. Realizing I was helpless to stop Technician 2 on my own, I escaped from our quarters to seek assistance...but was struck by several bullets in the process."

"God damn," Fuseli said. "But why would Technician 2 react in such a way?

Never mind...hold that thought. You and me will talk about this later. Are you sure you don't need medical assistance?"

"You need not worry."

Fuseli left the Liaison's side to go to Tarragon. "We'd better do something fast, before it realizes that Drang can shoot grenades."

"I was thinking the same."

"Can you see through the wall with your scope? And how about firing through the wall?"

"Probably, to the first," Tarragon said. "I doubt it, to the second."

"At least see if you can tell us where it is in there."

As Tarragon raised his Drang to eye level and adjusted its sighting screen, Fuseli turned back to the Liaison, who had glided closer behind him.

"Please," the Liaison said, "try to take Technician 2 alive. There is much I would like to ask. I am certain you would want this information, yourself."

"We will if we can," Fuseli said. "You hear that, Morris? If you think you can get a clean shot through the wall, go for one of the arms holding the Drang."

"Still doubt I can get through this wall material, but I hear you."

Fuseli addressed the Liaison again. "Do you have any security cameras in there we could access with our wrist comps?"

"I am sorry, Doctor...we did not permit the staff here to install cameras in our quarters."

"Of course you didn't."

"Got it on screen," Tarragon announced.

Fuseli moved in close to Tarragon for a peek. He hadn't seen inside the Coleopteroids' quarters before this, but then very few of the Base Gertrude staff had; not since the structures had been created. It was mostly one open room, and the rack-like constructions lining two of its walls might have caused one to mistake the room for a small warehouse space. On closer inspection, though, the racks looked like a cross between bunk beds and the cells of a wasp nest. These were the chambers into which the eleven typical Coleopteroids would crawl in order to rest—at least, before most of them had been annihilated in the accident. Where the Liaison slept, if it did sleep, was not apparent. Elsewhere in the room, bulky machinery stood against the other walls, along with gas cylinders and drums of chemicals, apparently, while unusual technology was arranged atop various work counters.

All of this appeared somewhat vague and shadowy on the screen, however; mostly sketched in as outlines. Against this dark background, though, Technician 2 stood out as a green-glowing figure like that of some ghost. Or rather, one small part of a ghost that possessed a seemingly endless number of bodies.

The figure had crouched down on its multiple-jointed legs, taking cover behind one of those machines pushed up against the walls. Around the edge of the machine, it poked out the business end of the Drang it had taken from Private Townsend.

"What do you think it's thinking?" Tarragon said.

"It's thinking it has nowhere left to go," said Fuseli. "So it has nothing left to lose. Listen, if a projectile can't get through the wall, how about a beam on highest setting?"

"Eh...I don't know. Worth a try, I guess." Tarragon toggled his weapon from solid projectile mode to energy bolt mode.

"But we're trying to take it alive." Fuseli twisted around to face Tamati. "Okay, Lieutenant?"

"If you say so," Tamati grumbled. "How about we shoot a gas grenade in there, then? Knock it out?"

"That might work, if I knew what kind of gas knocks out a Bedbug."

"Hey!" Tarragon blurted.

On his screen, another green-glowing shape lay on the floor closer to the tiered sleep chambers. In focusing on Technician 2, they had overlooked it before, plus this other figure's glow was more faint and flickering. However, as Fuseli stared into Tarragon's sighting screen, this second ghostly shape struggled painfully into a standing position.

"It's Technician 8," Fuseli said. "It's still alive!"

The fainter ghost began staggering in jerky movements in the direction of the partly-hidden figure of Technician 2.

"It's going after the shooter," Tarragon said.

Even as they realized what was happening, they saw that Technician 2 realized it, too. Its brightly-glowing figure rose up from behind the odd machine and swung the Drang at its badly wounded comrade.

"It's distracted," Fuseli snapped, "move in!"

Almost before Fuseli had even finished his command, Tarragon was already swinging his Drang away from the wall he'd been peering through and charging the room's open doorway. He plunged through it, and Tamati jumped in after Tarragon before Fuseli could do the same.

Tarragon lunged into the room in time to see Technician 2 unleash a stream of automatic fire at its dying comrade, before Technician 8 could take more than a few agonized steps. Its exoskeleton already punched through with holes, Technician 8 juddered in place as this new fusillade of bullets drilled through it, blowing shards of chitin out of its carapace.

Distracted by the dying Technician 8's attempt at revenge, Technician 2 noticed too late the humans pouring into the room. It started to turn, and in so doing swung its Drang around to fire at the Colonial Forcers instead, but not quickly enough. Tarragon came to an abrupt halt, and with two expert shots—his Drang still set to fire streaking white energy bolts—struck the Coleopteroid in both of its prosthetic arms that gripped the Drang. One of these limbs was sheared off completely, while the other swung by a tendon-like cable, sparks spitting out of it. The Drang clattered to the floor at its feet.

Through all this, Technician 2 made not a sound, but it bent in an effort to retrieve the fallen Drang with its two remaining prosthetic arms...one of them twitching continuously now. Before it could touch the gun, however, Tarragon was there and swinging the butt of his Drang up into the Coleopteroid's beetle-like face. It flew backwards, landing on its carapace.

Technician 2 thrashed wildly on its back, swinging its uppermost pair of limbs—those that hadn't been replaced by prosthetics—trying to lash at the men's legs with the pincers at their ends, but Tarragon took a stance again and squeezed off two more precise shots. This time, he severed the remaining pair of prosthetic arms neatly.

At that, Fuseli jumped in on one side, stomping on one tentacle-like limb and pinning it down. Tamati did the same on the other side. They both pointed their Drangs down at the Coleopteroid's glossy black head, with that odd gray splotch on the left side. Only then, looking up into the multiple muzzles of the formidable assault engines, did the Coleopteroid finally stop kicking and struggling.

Peripherally Fuseli saw other Colonial Forcers approaching, having entered the room in their wake, Private Sunday among them. Finally, trailing behind them came the Coleopteroid Liaison.

The Liaison stopped and towered over the captured Technician 2, gazing down at it with icy dispassion.

-17-

Fuseli did what he could for the injured Private Townsend, given the resources available, but he stressed to Dr. Marceau—who came to meet him in the med unit—that what the young man really needed was more extensive repair at someplace like Port Haven.

Now, together they walked back toward the Coleopteroids' living quarters, where the Liaison would be waiting for them. Dr. Mann, who had again assisted Fuseli while he tended to Townsend, hurried to catch up and accompany them. Fuseli had thought Mann would want to remain behind to run scans on the latest alternate that had been found, brought in while they were caring for Townsend. This one was already dead, after having materialized in the power plant. It was now mostly just a blob of gelatinous flesh, some areas cloudy white and others clear as glass, with several possible flippers or fins of a dark purple color. What it had looked like in life, they couldn't as yet say, but Mann's opinion was that this being had been adapted to the intense pressure of deep ocean waters, and being teleported to their environment had caused its tissues to explode. The body had, in fact, been discovered lying in a puddle of water. The power plant was being sterilized as a precaution, and the dead creature had been added to the collection stored in the med unit cryo chambers. Despite this prize, Mann obviously didn't want to miss out on what the Liaison had to tell them.

As they walked, Fuseli said to Marceau, "I've been meaning to ask...you did notify all staff of what's going on here, right? The full story? You said you were going to do a meeting over their wrist comps."

"I'm sorry I didn't include you in that," she said. Marceau looked more baggy-eyed and haggard by the hour, and her voice was in keeping with that. "Yes, I did."

"And? How did that go?"

She glanced at Mann, then heaved a weary sigh. "It was a mess. A hundred questions all at once, as I expected. Chaos."

"And the general feeling? Is your staff willing to stay here and take part in this exciting new area of study, or do they want off this God-forsaken ice ball?"

"As you know, the staff here is made up of all sorts of people from many fields. Naturally, a mechanic in the garage or even a hydroponics worker isn't going to have the same enthusiasm as one of our researchers."

"But more want out than want to stay...am I right?"

"Dr. Fuseli, these people signed contracts! They have an obligation to fulfill! I certainly understand the anxiety some are feeling, but the project goes on until I get the official word that we pull the plug...or at least, pull out to regroup and rethink."

They had passed the conventional barracks, and now came up on the Coleopteroids' living quarters. The room's door had been closed, and a pair of Colonial Forcers stood guard outside it. One of them nodded to Fuseli and without a word unlocked the door to give them access. The door slid aside, and Fuseli, Marceau, and Mann stepped into the large single room.

Right away, Fuseli was struck by the state of Technician 2. Its body was suspended in a clear cylinder filled with a faintly-luminous orange fluid, like an old biological specimen preserved in a bottle of alcohol. The base the cylinder rested on was apparently a machine that circulated air through the quietly burbling liquid, or otherwise kept Technician 2 alive. Thanks to the assistance of two of Mann's medical staff, the imprisoned Coleopteroid was now missing even the stumps of its four severed prosthetic arms, retaining only its uppermost, tentacle-like pair of arms and its more insect-like single pair of legs.

"So what's this?" Fuseli asked, as he and the others approached the Liaison. Also here already were the tech who had replaced Chawla, whose name he'd since learned was Yukimi Shimada, and two other techs of lesser rank. Shimada met his eyes with concern, as if trying to mutely convey some message to him. He took a mental note.

It was the Liaison who answered. "We are keeping Technician 2 properly contained until another party of our people arrives to replace those lost... whenever that can be arranged. When that ship departs again for Earth, it will take Technician 2 with it, to eventually be returned to our home world for further questioning and the appropriate punishment."

"But you indicated that you've learned some things from it already," Fuseli said.

"Yes, Dr. Fuseli. I have very important information to impart, in the interest of transparency. This matter will, I sincerely hope, not damage relations between our people."

"What are you saying?"

"You may recall that I told you I suspected we were drawing close to an answer in regard to the destruction of the teleportation lab. I will now reveal that my suspicion was that the cause of the power overload and subsequent explosion was sabotage."

"Oh!" Marceau exclaimed.

"However," the Liaison went on, "it was not immediately clear if this sabotage was perpetrated by one of your people, or one of ours. I'm sorry to say, we suspected the former...that the saboteur might be a terrorist who had infiltrated the staff here. After interrogating Technician 2, it is now clear that it was the saboteur all along. You see, more than once we speculated that the origin of the problem might lie with something we call navigation fluid, a substance of our own devising. We incorporate globes filled with this fluid in our own extradimensional transports. But whereas in our case, two globes filled with navigation fluid are incorporated directly into each tran, for this project we installed a pair not in the teleportation pod itself but within a wall panel in the research area..."

Fuseli thought he got the picture in regard to this mysterious navigation fluid, the recipe for which the Coleopteroids no doubt meant to keep proprietary. Thus, even if they helped the Earth Colonies develop their own means of teleportation, humans would still be reliant on the Coleopteroids to supply their secret concoction.

He didn't interrupt, though, and the Liaison continued, "Unfortunately—and I am ashamed of my oversight—on those occasions that it was suspected the navigation globes themselves might be responsible for the power surges, it was always Technician 2 who performed the diagnostics on them."

"And assured you everything was in order," said Fuseli.

"Correct."

"Now we know why Technician 2 conveniently wasn't in the dome when things went south. And its reason for causing this sabotage? Does its motivation have anything to do with it apparently being an alternate of Anthony Nguyen? When it encountered Nguyen, did that realization freak it out...set it off? Make it want to stop the experiments here?"

"Technician 2 has, as I say, confessed to sabotaging the research, but has been less forthcoming about motivation. Technician 2 and Anthony Nguyen may not be alternates, after all...but if so, perhaps Technician 2 has not realized it yet, or does not even care. I believe Technician 2 has not revealed its motivation because it is protecting others."

"Others, back home—your home?"

"Yes. I can think of several possibilities. Our people are not, as you might think, all united in our beliefs. We are not a hive mind. There is, for instance, a cult that worships an alleged alien entity called Ugghiutu, worshipped on a number of worlds by very different races. Ugghiutu is said to be a being of god-like power, and these fanatical cults strive to conjure Ugghiutu into manifesting on their own worlds, so that they might better commune with this entity. It is possible that Technician 2 tampered with this project's technology not to destroy it, but to open a portal through which Ugghiutu might be summoned here."

"Well that sounds lovely," Fuseli said.

"My God!" Mann gasped.

Fuseli turned to him. "I should hope not." He looked to the Liaison again. "And these other possibilities?"

"More mundane, but still concerning. That Technician 2 may simply belong to a political group that is opposed to cooperation with the Earth Colonies. There are such groups, who I am afraid see any race other than our own as inferior... fit only for study, or exploitation, rather than diplomacy and partnership. In any case, since we have yet to extract the full truth from Technician 2, his interrogation must be continued."

"Captain Fuseli," the technician Yukimi Shimada spoke up, "can I speak with you for a minute?"

Fuseli excused himself, then stepped across the room with Shimada, toward one of the honeycombed walls where the typical Coleopteroids used to nest. She didn't object when Marceau and Mann tagged along.

"Yes?" Fuseli said.

"Captain, the Liaison directed us in setting up that tank the prisoner is in, but I didn't realize at the time...I think it's being tortured in there. The Liaison speaks into a microphone when it's questioning the prisoner...it's a kind of chittering sound, untranslated, so none of us can understand it. The prisoner answers through a speaker in the same way. Anyway, when the prisoner doesn't answer the Liaison's question, or when it seems like the Liaison doesn't like the answer, the Liaison pushes a button on a remote or something—maybe inside their robe—and electricity shoots through the fluid the prisoner is in, very plainly. I'm sorry, sir, but I can't assist it anymore if that's what it's going to do."

"We can't impose our own morals on another race," Fuseli said.

"Not even on our property?"

"I know this is complex..."

"Well, I won't have my morals imposed upon, either, Captain."

"I respect your feelings, Shimada. But, we need to know this thing's motivations. If it was trying to summon some...I don't know, superior god-like being here from another dimension, we kind of need to know if that's still a possibility."

"Can't they continue that questioning back home, like the Liaison says? In the mean time, I'd just as soon pull out of this place. My team feels the same."

Fuseli looked over at Marceau. She shook her head violently, one palm pressed to her forehead. "I keep saying, not until we get orders to do so...*if* we get orders to do so! I get it that this is an extraordinary situation and people are feeling nervous!"

"Imperiled, is the better word," said Fuseli.

"I won't take part in any further torture," Shimada repeated. "If the Liaison needs anything else done with the tank the prisoner is in, let it do it itself! I'm not military—you can't order me!"

"I'm afraid I can," Fuseli said. "But I won't. Come on." He led the little group back to the Liaison, standing in front of that softly burbling, orange-glowing tank in which Technician 2 stared out at them inscrutably. To the Liaison, he said, "Were these navigation globes destroyed in the blast, or what?"

"In fact, no. They remained intact, shielded as they were within their wall panel."

"So, they're still active. And are they still in communication with the teleportation pod?"

"They would still be linked, in the most basic way."

"Could the fact that the pod and globes are still active be the reason this rift is still open...alternates still passing through it?"

The Liaison demonstrated one of those long pauses in which it seemed to think deeply...or in which it seemed hesitant to answer. "That may well be the case."

"Then we need to make them fully inactive, even if that means destroying the globes and the pod. To close the rift, if that's possible."

"Dr. Fuseli, I forbid it!" Marceau cried.

"You can't!" Mann cried. "We've been over and over how important this new line of research could be! Even for *you!*" He pointed at the Liaison.

"You'd better call your General Stroud," Marceau said, "because you're out of your depth, Dr. Fuseli—with all respect—and I will not accept that order from you!"

Fuseli shifted one step closer to Marceau, and said, "If I were to deem it necessary, and you didn't want to cooperate, I'd have my Colonial Forcers go into your lab and set up another nice big explosion. This time with the teleportation pod inside, and those two navigation globes resting on its seat."

"The military," she spat, visibly shaking. "All you know is destroying."

"I'll make that call to General Stroud," Fuseli told her. "Rest assured. In the meantime, we don't need to destroy anything in your precious lab...but we will uninstall those navigation globes, and power down that pod one hundred percent." He addressed Shimada. "Get your people on that. And that *is* an order."

"You don't have to order me," Shimada said. "I'll do it."

To Marceau again, Fuseli said, "If the upper-ups tell Stroud that we're to power those things up again, it can be done easily enough. But for now, better safe than sorry...even if I'm wrong and that doesn't close the rift."

"It might indeed close the rift," Mann objected, "but who knows what combination of factors is at work here? Reinstalling the globes and powering the pod up again might not reopen the rift! It could be lost to us forever!"

"That's a risk I'll take," Fuseli said, "rather than the risk that more staff will be hurt and killed."

"I will oversee the removal of the navigation globes," the Liaison spoke up. "I can instruct your technicians what to do."

"Thank you," Fuseli said.

"I agree," the Liaison went on, "that prudence is best. After all, who can say whether this rift, which we know so little about and cannot even pinpoint, might tear open wider...and wider."

Even Marceau and Mann just gaped in silence at that possibility.

-18-

In his quarters, Fuseli linked his wrist comp with the mounted wall screen so he could speak with General Stroud, back at Port Haven, more comfortably. He sat on the edge of his bed, holding a coffee he'd grabbed from the cafeteria. With it, he'd washed down another stimulant pill. He thought just about everybody at Base Gertrude could benefit from one of those about now.

Having been fully updated, General Aaron Stroud drew in a long, slow breath and let it out in the same way. "Okay, Bob, so let's hear what you propose, in detail."

"Right," Fuseli said. "It's this. First, we do what's already being done as we speak...uninstall their navigation globes, and shut that pod down *cold.* Then, we make as much food as we can, quickly, in the cafeteria and leave it out on the tables in case more alternates show up after we go. They have the hydroponics garden, too, and access to water. We leave the base power on, and all life support systems active—air, artificial gravity. We leave all the robots up and running, to help maintain things and so we can monitor the base through their eyes. Then, we evacuate the entire staff, right down to the Liaison and Tech 2. We have a number of pilots stationed on base, plus Halabi and Rix who flew me here. If we spread them out, they should be enough to pilot the base's various vessels out there on the launch pads."

"You may not have enough for a copilot on every vessel."

"Not ideal, I know, but it isn't like we'd be traveling far...not to Port Haven, but for now just to Port Urano, in orbit around Uranus. I know a gas operation isn't exactly a hotel, but there should be enough room there for people to wait until they can get shuttled elsewhere...even if they have to sleep on the floor for a while."

"Why not Base Urano, on Titania itself? It's only, what, twenty miles from your location?"

"Twenty-three. Well, we could, but I'd just feel better being off this ball of ice altogether right now."

On screen, Stroud chewed his upper lip, taking it all in. "Sounds good, but of course I need to take this upstairs. And Bob, I have to say...maybe you were a bit premature in having the techs remove those globes and shut down the pod."

"Unless the rift did tear wider, if we left them in," Fuseli said. "In which case, it should have been done a lot sooner."

"True enough. Well, I'll be conferring with technical people on my end, too...see what they think of everything in light of new information."

"I'll take good care of those balls, don't worry," Fuseli assured him. "As good as I take care of my own."

"All right, Bob. I'll be back with you ASAP, about your proposal."

"Thanks, General."

The screen went dark. Reflected in it, as if in a dark mirror, Fuseli saw Rhan

Luyen standing behind him in his room's open doorway. Somewhat startled, he got to his feet and faced her.

Smiling, Rhan inclined her head toward the coffee in his hand. "And here I was just about to invite you to go grab a coffee with me."

"We can still go get one for you."

"I'll just have a sip of yours, if that's okay."

Fuseli blinked...then went to her, handed over his coffee, and watched the woman take a slow sip, her eyes on his all the while. As she lowered the cup, she said, "Surprised to see me out of my prison cell? Don't worry—the guard's still out there in the hall. I just told him I needed some air." She snorted. "Some air. God, I never thought I'd miss that shitty little town of mine so much. Not too many trees here on Titania."

"Sit down," Fuseli invited her. He went to the little chair near the flip-down desk, while she sat on the edge of his bed, still holding onto his coffee, as if duplicating his pose of just seconds ago.

Rhan glanced around his mostly empty room. "Yours isn't much different from mine. I guess we're all just prisoners of one kind or another."

"That's an odd thing to say. You're not a prisoner...not here, anyway. So, have you ever been in one, like our friend Tony Nguyen?"

She rolled his coffee cup between her palms. "Now *that's* an odd thing to say."

"What do you think of him...your double from another mother?"

"I don't like him at all. He's a smug idiot. He tried speaking Vietnamese to me. I'm not Vietnamese. What do you think of him?"

"Not much. I suppose he has a certain charm. Many criminals do."

"And what do you think of me...Robert?"

"I like you better than him. But there are things you won't tell me, and that's a bit frustrating. Why so adamant about not taking a truth scan?"

"I don't want my privacy violated. You can't make me." She looked back up at him. "Can you?"

"I can...but I won't. Or at least, I hope I never have to."

"I understand it would be crazy to think I could get back home...and to tell you the truth, now I don't want to. When you take me to your Earth, will you see to it personally I'm set up okay, to start a new life?"

"Yes. I'll see to it you're treated right. Though, I'm pretty sure no one's going to let a person from a parallel universe just step out of the ship and wave goodbye and walk off into the sunset. There are going to be a lot of interviews with a lot of different interviewers. Wherever they settle you, people are going to want access to you for a long time."

"I can understand that. I just...I just hope I can have my freedom, in general. Not be kept in a cell most the time like I am here. And...God..." She started nervously rolling the coffee cup again.

"And what?"

"I suppose I should tell you. They'll get it out of me sooner or later, truth scan or no."

"You can talk to me, Rhan. Like I said, I'll see that you're taken care of, with consideration and respect. But the more honest you are with me, the better I'll be able to advocate for you."

Rhan stood, walked to him, handed him back his coffee. Then, she began to pace in his room as she spoke, like a leopard restless in its cage. "I lied when I said I was in the prosthetics factory when I felt dizzy and passed out, before I woke up here. I *used* to work there, but that was before...before what sent me to prison. I was in my cell when it happened. I got lightheaded and had to sit down, and the rest was like I said. Huh...I wonder if my bunkie saw it happen, and what she thought of it. What they *all* thought of it. The ultimate jailbreak."

"So what did you go to prison for, Rhan?"

"I told you, I made bad choices in life. Maybe my worst choice was having a kid...sticking her with *me* for a mother. Then again, she's the best thing that ever happened to me. But, a definite bad choice I made was cheating on her dad. That's why he left me. After that, I got involved with some bad people. Doing drugs, selling drugs. And then I met this one guy. That asshole Nguyen reminds me of him. One night, when I had my daughter over for the weekend, the both of us got drunk...and while I was passed out, my boyfriend...he..." She stopped pacing.

"He abused her."

"I should have gone to the police," she whispered, gazing at a blank wall, as if through it she could observe herself in the past, but was helpless to advise that earlier version of Rhan Luyen and change her fate.

"What did you do to him?"

"He kept a handgun in our apartment. After what my daughter told me...oh God, she was *crying*...crying and hugging me...she was only twelve years old then! I went into our room and woke him up, and I waited until he was awake enough to see what I was going to do, and then I shot him right in his fucking dick. And then, after I let him think about that for a couple seconds, I shot him in the face."

"I see," Fuseli said softly.

She turned to face him again, her eyes filmed with tears that she stubbornly managed to keep from spilling. "You must have killed people, as a soldier."

"Plenty."

"Do you regret any of them?"

Without hesitation, Fuseli said, "No. I never killed anyone who didn't deserve it. At least to my mind."

"I feel the same," Rhan said. "At least to my mind. I regret not being with my daughter after that, and I regret that I ever got involved with that guy, but I don't regret what I did to him. Though...I suppose, if you think about it, isn't it better that I was already out of my daughter's life when I was sucked into this place? Imagine if she was with me when that happened...even *saw* it happen? It would have been more painful for her then. Though now, she may go the rest of her life not knowing where I disappeared to. Not knowing will always haunt her."

Fuseli stood up from his chair, went to her, touched her arm lightly. "Many a parent would have done the same thing you did. Or would want to, at least."

"Oh yeah? You mean, you don't see me as just another sinful version of the same person, like Nguyen and all these monsters pouring into this base?"

"None of them are monsters. I'm sure there are those people who think of me as a monster, for things I've had to do. In fact, I know there are."

"You don't think I'll be imprisoned in your world, for what I did in mine?"

"No. I just think, at most, people will want to keep a close eye on you for a while, but not in the sense of jailers. They would anyway, without even knowing what you did."

"Do you have to tell them?" She put her hand over his, where it rested on her arm.

"Yes. I'm sorry, but I do."

Fuseli expected Rhan to remove her hand from his then, and even to step back away from him. Instead, she moved even closer, tilting her face up to his.

Fuseli put his arms around her, and their mouths found each other. They kissed deeply, and it was good, but then he remembered the open door. What if the guard posted out there, checking on Rhan, were to come over and peek in? But Rhan sensed his distraction, glanced behind her and caught on. She slipped out of his arms, went to the door and locked it. Then she turned to face him...still with her eyes gleaming moistly, but smiling, and undoing the top of her bright yellow scrubs.

-19-

Yukimi Shimada herself removed the second of the pair of navigation globes, delicately as if it were a fragile glass sphere filled with luminous milky-white fluid. It was that, actually, though how fragile the sphere itself might be she didn't want to test. Under the watchful eyes of the Liaison, who stood behind her, she moved the globe to a container on a cart minded by one of her assistants, and lowered it into a recessed space. The assistant tech closed the container's lid, and locked it.

"We have a new visitor," said the Liaison, without any urgent inflection in its voice, but Shimada looked up with a start and spun around.

A man stood only paces away, as if he too had been watching the operation all this time, as the navigation globes were removed from behind their panel in the dome's curved, fire-blackened wall. He was taller than Anthony Nguyen but still of slender build, and while his features were very similar to Nguyen's they were perhaps more sleek and refined in their cut. He did not, however, share a port-wine stain on the left side of his face. Rather like the Liaison, the man had no hair, no eyebrows or eyelashes, but black makeup like kohl outlined his eyes, with long tails extending from their corners. His skin was not just pale, but the bright white of paper, while the irises of his eyes were crimson. The stranger wore an outfit that might call to mind pajamas of lustrous silver silk, embroidered with a pattern of flowers—or might they be some type of jellyfish or tentacled mollusk?—in metallic red thread to match his eyes.

The man smiled at Shimada, nodded at the container on the cart, and asked in a subtly synthetic voice, "What is it you're doing there? What is this place?"

"Hey!" cried one of the two Colonial Forcers who guarded the room, and the teleportation pod specifically. Having heard people speaking, he'd casually looked behind him and spotted this stranger who had appeared in the dome out of nowhere. As he strode toward them, the C-Forcer leveled his Drang threateningly. "Don't you move!"

"I would advise you not to attempt violence toward me," said the man with crimson eyes.

"I would advise you to shut your mouth and put your hands over your head!"

The other Colonial Forcer posted in the dome was coming on the heels of the first. He snarled, "You heard the man, baldy!"

The smile of the man with crimson eyes only grew wider. "Oh, what abysmal place is this I've been summoned to?" With that, faster than the human eye could follow he had reached out a hand and caught Shimada by the front of her collar, jerking her almost off her feet and closer to him. Stepping behind her, using her as a shield, with his other hand he produced a dagger from somewhere. The dagger's glassy blade looked to be made from ruby or some sort of red crystal, again to complement his eyes, and he pressed its tip under Shimada's jaw...with enough pressure to instantly draw a bead of blood.

"Don't do it!" the first Colonial Forcer yelled, halting his advance but raising his assault engine to his shoulder and looking into his sighting screen. "I've got your head dead in my sights! I'll take it off at the shoulders if you don't put that fucking knife down *now!*"

"Why the animosity, friend?" asked the stranger. Not only did his voice sound strangely artificial, but the movement of his lips and the words he spoke didn't quite match up. "I didn't ask to come here. Apparently you've summoned me, and all I was doing was asking this creature why."

Shimada looked terrified, and yet she held out a palm to warn the two Colonial Forcers to stay their trigger fingers. "Don't, please! Let's talk to him! Please, just call Dr. Marceau!"

"Fuck that," said the second C-Forcer to the first, lowering his Drang to use his wrist comp. "I'm calling Captain Fuseli."

Fuseli awoke with a start, and the first thing he felt was stupidity, for having fallen asleep beside Rhan Luyen. He believed he knew her much better now, but it was still more than imprudent to have let his guard down this much. She had, after all, admitted to him she was a murderer. What had awakened him, though, was not Rhan attacking him when he was vulnerable but slipping out of bed, naked like himself, and walking toward the door to her room. She started reaching out to the door controls...

Fuseli hurried out of bed, leaped after Rhan and caught her by the arms from behind, shifting him around to face him. "Hey, hey," he chuckled nervously, "what do you think you're doing...going out there to parade your glory for the whole base to see?"

She looked into his eyes dully, as if she barely recognized him. "Someone's calling me."

"Calling you? No one's calling you, my dear—you were dreaming. Apparently, you still are."

"I'm not dreaming," she murmured, twisting around in his arms without actually struggling against him, to gaze at the room's closed door. "Don't you hear it?"

"I don't hear anything. I'm telling you, you're sleepwalking."

"No. It's a voice. It's in my head. Yeah...that's why *you* can't hear it. It's...the Man from the Plain."

"The Plain?" Fuseli guided her back toward the bed. "Listen, Rhan, if you want to go outside at least put some clothes on."

Instead, Rhan crawled back into bed and pulled the covers over her again, now looking like a timid child shaken by a nightmare. "You're right...I don't want to go to the voice. I don't trust him."

"You don't trust...the Man from the Plain?"

"Yes."

Fuseli gathered up his clothing, started dressing. "I've been here too long. I need to go look in on things, and you need to go back to sleep for a bit, I'd say."

"Do you have to leave me?"

The fear she was exhibiting disturbed him. This wasn't like Rhan at all; at least the Rhan he had come to know thus far. Had her confession shattered a tough veneer too long under internal strain? "I'll be back to look in on you later, okay? But I do need to go."

"Please come back as soon as you can, Robert."

"I promise, Rhan."

With the Colonial Forcers spread thin, patrolling the base on the lookout for the appearance of more alternates, plus guarding the dome, there was only one man stationed in the hallway outside the rooms of Anthony Nguyen and Rhan Luyen. When Fuseli emerged from Rhan's room, thinking he'd head to the showers before he went to check on the techs' progress in the dome, the solitary guard looked at him and wagged his head.

"Sir, if I might speak freely...you had me pretty worried when you didn't come out of there. I was thinking I should check in on you, but I was afraid to... um...bother you."

"Sorry, private. Didn't mean to worry you. I worry myself sometimes, too."

"I thought she might have killed you or something."

"Well, my heart almost did give out once or twice," Fuseli muttered, looking down at his wrist comp as a number of calls started coming in, clamoring for his attention. "Oh man...this can't be good."

-20-

Olivia Marceau had been in the ancillary lab nearest to the dome, disabling any processes that had a remote connection to the teleportation pod and the housing for the navigation globes. Thus, on a monitor before her she happened to see the eerie stranger talking with Shimada...and then seizing her, taking her as a hostage, when the two security people trained their guns on him.

Being closer to the dome than Fuseli, Marceau got there first.

She approached the tense standoff with her hands held up so the hairless stranger with his uncanny paper-white skin could see she was unarmed. "Lower your guns!" she called to the two Colonial Forcers as she came. "You heard me!"

The two C-Forcers glanced at each other, then lowered their Drangs from their shoulders but kept them pointed at the stranger from waist level. Marceau moved past them, and faced the man with crimson eyes.

"Sorry to say, it doesn't surprise me that I would be greeted with such barbarism among creatures like you," he said, but all the while maintaining his pleasant smile—and maintaining the pressure of his dagger's point under Shimada's jaw. A trickle of blood was winding down her taut throat, looking like an external vein. "Am I to take it you're in charge here?"

"I am," Marceau said. "I'm Dr. Olivia Marceau—I'm the head of this research project."

"Research into what?"

"Teleportation."

The man with crimson eyes nodded at the bathysphere-like teleportation pod on its raised central platform. "Teleportation in *that* primitive contraption?"

"Primitive?" said the Liaison, with the barest hint of surprise in its monotone of a voice. Or was it even indignation?

The stranger addressed the Liaison. "Are you a synthetic?"

"Do you mean, an automaton? I am not. I am a member of the race these beings call the Coleopteroids, modified into a state that is easier for them to communicate with. My race has been assisting them in developing teleportation."

"Well, it would seem to me that the research you are assisting them with has inadvertently summoned me here."

"That is in fact the case, regrettably," said the Liaison.

"Oh...regrettably doesn't begin to cover it," said the man with crimson eyes. He tilted his chin up a bit, his eyes flicking to and fro as if he were suddenly listening to sounds none of the rest of them could hear.

Marceau said, "You seem to be a very advanced being, so you must realize we mean you no harm."

"*Seem* to be advanced?"

"Please let my colleague go. We're happy to talk with you, and help you in any way we can."

"Help me get back to my world, in that sad monstrosity? I highly doubt it."

"What is your world? And what is your name?"

"Shh." The man with crimson eyes continued listening, but then said, "My name is Yarlath. I come from the Plane."

"The...Plane?"

"I am sensing a number of iterations of myself in this complex. And one outside it...a quite large one. None of them feel familiar to me, however, in terms of their race. Close by, there is a man...and a woman. There is another one confined to...a bottle, it would seem. I also sense the trace energies of several dead iterations."

"Oh my God," Marceau said. "So you're familiar with this phenomenon of alternate versions of yourself? And you can even sense them?"

"I am quite familiar. In fact, another iteration of myself accompanied me here. Unfortunately, it was received inside that teleportation conveyance of yours, instead of outside it like myself."

"It accompanied you here?"

"Yes...it's been my Companion for some time."

The two Colonial Forcers suddenly switched their attention to the pod. "There's something in there, too?" one of them demanded.

"I would be obliged," said Yarlath, "if you would free my Companion now."

"We aren't to open that pod!' the other Colonial Forcer snapped.

The Man from the Plane increased pressure against Shimada's throat, inserting the very tip of his blade under the skin. She cried out. "I must insist," he said.

"I'll do it!" Marceau blurted. "Please, don't hurt her...I'll open it!" She hurried toward the pod's platform.

"Dr. Marceau!" one of the guards cried. "Captain Fuseli has ordered everyone not to open that pod!"

"I'm in charge of this base, not Dr. Fuseli!" said Marceau, rushing past him and mounting the platform's stairs. She went to the pod's curved door to manually input the control panel's password to unlock it, since the pod had been powered down and couldn't be controlled from her wrist comp.

"Doctor!" cried the other guard. "Check the camera first to see what's inside!"

Marceau didn't listen, and punched in the code's last number just as Captain Robert Fuseli came running into the dome, with Morris Tarragon and Rhys Tamati behind him...Fuseli having called them on his wrist comp while on the way.

Also just as Marceau was punching in the last number, the pod rocked on its platform slightly, with a great thud that came from within. The sound and the pod's violent shudder caused Marceau to jolt back, shocked. That anything within could be strong enough to cause the heavy metal sphere to quake like that...

The door slid open, and unfolding from within came the Companion of the Man from the Plane.

"What are you doing there?" Fuseli shouted to Marceau, too late.

"Don't shoot it!" she yelled. She was so quick to retreat from the platform that she nearly dropped off onto her back. "He has a knife to Yukimi's throat!"

"Jesus Christ!" Tamati said, pointing his sidearm in both hands to steady himself.

"Hold off," Fuseli said, his attention flicking to the Man from the Plane and then back to the thing that emerged from the teleportation pod. Like Tamati, he and Tarragon had their Scythe handguns trained on the Companion.

"It will do what I will it to do," Yarlath told them. "No more...and no less."

The Companion was very like a chimpanzee, if any still existed at this time, but lacking all hair whatsoever—and thus, all of its body's powerful muscles were starkly delineated. Unlike a chimp, when it finally stood mostly upright after squeezing out of the pod, the creature was nearly seven feet in height, and its skin was as crimson as the eyes of the Man from the Plane...whether naturally or dyed. Fuseli wondered about the latter, because against this striking field of red the proto-human had been tattooed from its jug-eared head to its prehensile feet with a pattern identical to that with which Yarlath's pajama-like outfit was embroidered: something like a flower or sea creature, except here rendered in black ink instead of red thread.

The Companion's eyes, entirely black, shot fury at first one of the humans gathered there and then the next, and the next, as if taking a count, its huge fists clenching so tight that one might have heard their bones crackle.

"If you have any control of that thing and you don't want it dead," Fuseli shouted, "you'd better tell it not to step off that platform!"

"I would be more willing to agree to your request, friend," said Yarlath, "if you people would only just stop pointing your crude weapons at us."

"And you had better take your crude weapon away from that woman's throat!"

"It's unfortunate the position we find ourselves in here, I do admit. If only I had been greeted with anything but savagery from you people from the moment I arrived here—against my will."

"Tell me who you are," Fuseli demanded, not taking his eyes off the Companion. And either because he was the one shouting, or because the thing could work out that he was the one in charge, the Companion had settled its enraged eyes on him.

"As I told this rather more sensible woman, here, who released my Companion...my name is Yarlath. I come from the Plane."

"The Plane," Fuseli repeated to himself. He remembered what Rhan had said...

"And where is this Plane? What is it?"

"It is the place you sad children ripped me from with your experiments, it would appear. Both me and my Companion."

"How is that possible, that your pet here was teleported with you?"

"His Companion is an alternate version of him!" Marceau told Fuseli. "In Yarlath's world, they're aware of their alternates...and he can even sense those who came here ahead of him. I think he's in telepathic communication with them."

"Is that so?" Fuseli asked Yarlath. "You tell this thing what to do telepathically?"

"Our minds are linked," Yarlath confirmed. "And being that my Companion's mind is so very primitive—even less so than your own—he is easy to master. Ah... but if only I could master your minds, and compel you to put your toys away! Unfortunately, we from the Plane are only able to control our own iterations. Strange, that...we barely understand it ourselves."

"Well that is interesting," Fuseli said. "And I, in turn, can barely explain to you how you came to be here. Believe me, I'd rather you hadn't, just as much as you do."

"I hardly think you could regret this development as I do," said Yarlath. "If your experiments are out of control—and from the looks of this room, very much out of control—I would assume you are not in a position to return me to my own world."

"Look...Mr. Yarlath," Marceau said imploringly, stepping closer to him. "Honestly, we should all just talk! Starting by all of us putting our weapons away! If you have knowledge of your alternates in your world, and can even meet them, then obviously your people are capable of extradimensional teleportation...so maybe you can help us with our research here! Help us find a way to improve our own methods, so you can eventually return to the Plane!"

Yarlath cocked his head at her, as if amused by some notion a child had suggested to him. "Madam...I myself am no scientist. Not to sell myself short, of course, but it simply isn't my field."

"But you're clearly highly advanced..."

"At least now you say *clearly* instead of *seem*."

"Yes! So there has to be information you can share about your world's technology, even if your understanding of it is only basic." Marceau looked around at Fuseli, her eyes desperately hopeful. "Just think of the things we can learn from him!"

"I'd be happy to learn from him," Fuseli said, "if only he'd let Shimada go, and tell his Companion here to get back into that pod so we can lock it up again."

"Aren't you afraid of the damage he might cause in there?" Yarlath asked innocently. "Really, as you are my hosts, I must insist that if one side here is to end this stalemate, it must be yours. After all, as I have said, I exhibited no hostility until these two soldiers here came at me with their weapons pointed at my face."

"Dr. Fuseli!" Marceau cried. "All of you Colonial Forces people have got to put your weapons down! I suggest everyone leave but you, and that you put your gun back in its holster."

"Not going to happen, with that thing there ready to jump on me," Fuseli said. "Okay...look, Mr. Yarlath from the Plane. I'll tell these two soldiers to leave. The three of us here will lower our pistols, but we won't put them away. That's the best I can do. In return, you take that knife away from Shimada's throat. And your pet can remain free...for the moment."

Yarlath heaved a dramatic sigh. "Dealing with you primates is so very humiliating. But...I suppose we can't go on like this forever, can we? Very well... Dr. Fuseli, is it? Tell those two soldiers of yours to leave this room, for a start."

"You sure, Captain?" Tamati said in a low voice.

"Stay ready to shoot that Companion of his in the face if it makes one move toward us."

"Oh, count on it."

"Okay!" Fuseli said. "You two men...lower the Drangs and wait outside this room."

"Yes, Captain." Giving Yarlath, and then his Companion, one last threatening look, the two Colonial Forces guards turned and walked to the dome's primary entrance. After they had passed through it, its door slid shut again.

"I appreciate the concession," said Yarlath. He put his lips close to Shimada's ear. "I apologize for my rudeness, madam." He removed the blade of his red crystal knife from her neck, which by now was streaked with a ribbon of blood. When he released his hold on her, she spun and darted away from him with a gasped sob. The other techs who had been working with Shimada put her behind them protectively.

"Go to the med unit, Shimada," Fuseli said, eyes still locked on the Companion. Throughout all this, the proto-human had remained dead quiet, and that was as disturbing to him as anything else about it. "And you techs, leave...go with her."

They looked only too happy to oblige. In a moment, the only people who remained within the dome were Fuseli, Marceau, Tarragon, Tamati, and the Liaison...and Yarlath and his Companion. The three Colonial Forces men lowered their Scythes to their sides, but didn't return them to their holsters. Yarlath did, however, return his knife to a sheath beneath the hem of his top.

"Well then," said the Man from the Plane, spreading his arms. "Let us talk."

-21-

Dr. Mann had arrived in the hallway outside the locked rooms of test subject Anthony Nguyen and unwilling visitor Rhan Luyen as quickly as he could, upon being summoned by the solitary guard presently stationed there.

"Have you notified Dr. Fuseli?" Mann asked the guard, as he came huffing down the corridor.

"No, sir; he responded to an emergency," the guard replied.

Mann came to a stop. "Emergency? What emergency?"

"I don't know, sir."

"I'd better find out. But what's going on with—"

Before Mann could finish, a loud pounding came from within Anthony Nguyen's room. He was apparently banging on the locked door. His voice could be heard raging through it, as well.

"He's been doing that for about ten minutes...not sure why," the guard reported. "I didn't want to go in there until I got someone from med unit down here. He's sounding pretty crazy."

"Huh," Mann said. "All right...open it for me. Let's see what's going on."

The guard punched a code to unlock the door, then moved aside for Mann as it slid open.

Just beyond the doorway, Anthony Nguyen stood there looking wild-eyed, a trickle of blood running from his nose. A goose egg stood out on his forehead, and Mann wondered if it was his head Nguyen had been banging on the inner door, and not his fists. The blood he couldn't account for.

"What is it, Mr. Nguyen? The guard says you've been carrying on."

"What are you people doing to me?" Nguyen hissed through gritted teeth.

"What do you mean?"

Nguyen started forward as if to step out of his room, but the guard raised his Drang a bit to point from the hip. "Easy there, pal."

"This voice in my head!" Nguyen snarled. "What is it? How are you doing that?"

"I assure you, Mr. Nguyen, no one's doing anything to you," said Mann. "What is it, this voice in your head? Is it saying something?"

"And the dream I was having." Nguyen looked over his shoulder nervously, as if he expected to see some solid manifestation from his dream in the room's corners, having followed him here from the other side of sleep.

"Well that explains it," Mann said. "It seems to me you were just having a bad dream."

Nguyen wagged his head, still looking behind him suspiciously as he sought to recall his dream...or vision. "I was looking at the sky. It looked...fucked up. And these things were floating up there...like giant jellyfish. Opening and closing...or something like that. Glowing red. They were making a pattern in the sky. Yeah...a circle, right above me. Like they were smart. Like they were *watching* me."

"That definitely does sound like quite the dream," Mann chuckled. "Is that where the voice came from? The jellyfish?"

"No." Nguyen looked Mann in the face again. "The voice was from the man with red eyes. The...Man from the Plane."

"From the *Plane?*"

"He looked like me! But he wasn't me. He was a...a *demon.*"

"I see. A demon. And what was this demon saying to you, then?"

"To come to him," Nguyen whispered, as if he were afraid to reveal it. "Come to him and serve him."

"How is it you know our language?" Marceau asked Yarlath.

"I don't," he said. "It's just a trick I'm playing on you. I'm speaking my language, but you're hearing your own language in your heads."

"Ah! Of course—I see it now! Seeing you speak, it's like watching a really old movie that was dubbed into English!"

"Yes," the Liaison confirmed. "I am also hearing you in the language of my race, which these humans cannot comprehend."

"I thought you said you're only telepathic with your alternate selves," Fuseli said.

Yarlath held up a finger. "*No*, that's not what I said. I said I can *control* only my iterations, not that I can't communicate directly with your minds. Well, that is to say, I still need to vocalize to make the trick work. But as to why I can't control you also, as I do my Companion...well, this appears to be something my kind imposed on itself generations ago; something instituted by our culture to prevent us from trying to dominate others besides our personal iterations. Perhaps that deep-seated conditioning could be unlearned, if only we tried."

"So you've understood teleportation for quite a long time," Marceau said, her eyes all but sparkling with wonder.

"Yes. We make free use of it."

"How is it my kind has never crossed paths with yours before?" asked the Liaison.

"I might ask the same of you," said Yarlath. "But then, there are infinite realities."

Listening to Yarlath and Marceau converse, while still keeping his attention mostly on that hulking crimson-skinned simian, Fuseli found his thoughts straying to Rhan. Sleepwalking, so it appeared...answering the call of the "Man from the Plane." Compelled to obey, but at the same time frightened of obeying. And here was Yarlath, boasting how he could control alternate versions of himself. Had Yarlath been calling to Rhan unconsciously, or only too consciously?

"So your Companion here, who you see as a lesser being than yourself—" he began.

"Do you not see him as a lesser being than I?" said Yarlath. "Do you not acknowledge he is a lesser being than *yourself*? It's simply stating an undeniable reality."

"But what is it you make him do for you? Or any other of these 'iterations' of yourself you control?"

"The various uses to which our iterations can be put depends on how many you've had the opportunity to gather, and how many your household can support. There, they might do any number of things for you, depending on their particular skills or abilities. This Companion, who I'm particularly fond of, is of course not good for too much himself, except to perform heavy labor, but primarily I find him...entertaining."

"What do the others do for you? Just how many races have you met that were iterations of your kind?"

"Oh, a good many. I certainly can't say that my household supports a representative of every one of them."

"But you're saying you make these beings into slaves. Because you see them as inferior."

"The very fact that we can control them proves that they *are* inferior, Dr. Fuseli. It is again a simple fact that my kind has never...*never* encountered another sentient race that was *not* inferior to us."

"And so you feel entitled to do anything you want with them."

"Again, I stress...only with our own personal iterations. You see, because they are *us*...we *own* them. They are only extensions of ourselves...the way your own fingernails are not your mind. Your teeth serve you, but they can be extracted, and you will only have removed a minor portion of the whole of your being—because you own *yourself*."

"Each iteration of you is its own being! With its own mind, and experiences and feelings!"

"Yes. And yet, no. Just because your heart is beating without your conscious effort—as if it were not even aware of what we're discussing right now—does not mean that it is not an extension of you. It carries on in its own way, as does your digestive system, while your mind—the superior and dominant portion of you—carries on in its own way, and..."

"We're talking about *multiple* minds here, not *one* mind."

"Ugh...here I am trapped in this hell," Yarlath sighed, "arguing ethics. Please listen, Dr. Fuseli...I myself do not treat my iterations poorly. Yes, there are those of my kind who, for instance, find it amusing to release their collection into a designated hunting area, and killing them off for sport. Just as there are others among us who use certain types of iterations as livestock. And there are even factions, I will admit, who are so offended by the inferiority of these races that they advocate for annihilating any iterations of ourselves we should encounter in our extradimensional explorations. But I, myself, am of a benevolent nature. I treat the lesser aspects of myself quite well...so long as they don't defy me."

Fuseli glanced over at Marceau, to see how she was reacting to all this, but she just appeared to be listening with rapt fascination. He didn't feel he had to take his eyes off the proto-human and glance at Tarragon to know what his old friend was thinking.

Then, he noticed that the Companion was becoming aroused, while it continued to silently glare at him, its breathing through its nostrils growing faster and more shallow, the muscles in its heavy lower jaw tightening. He nodded at the creature.

"Why is that happening...can you tell me?"

Yarlath looked where Fuseli indicated, and snorted. "Ah, well...don't you find that rage and arousal are closely linked, Dr. Fuseli?"

"No. I do not. I don't think that's a natural reaction. I think it's something he's learned from you."

Yarlath narrowed his eyes slightly. "Can we talk, now, about what you suggest I do now that I've been marooned here? My polite manner may not be a true indication of just how perturbed I really am. I can assure you, Doctor, that I am *highly* perturbed by what has happened to me."

Marceau spoke up. "Just a moment after you arrived, we shut down the equipment we believe may have been maintaining the rift that was inadvertently opened when our project was...well, it was sabotaged by an iteration of yourself. A terrorist, that we now have confined. We have no way of knowing, just yet, if that will work and the rift has truly been closed."

"One of my iterations, a terrorist? Well, how dreadful."

"But," Marceau continued, "we're waiting for our superiors to determine our next course of action. Any way you look at it, though, these experiments with teleportation must continue...and when they do, I promise you one of the things we'll be working on is to get you back home. And, worst case scenario, if my people can't deliver on that, perhaps the Coleopteroids can." She gestured at the Liaison.

For its part, the Liaison did not agree or disagree in regard to Marceau's suggestion that its kind might assist Yarlath in returning to the place he called the Plane. The Liaison went on quietly watching Yarlath, as if mulling over its own private thoughts.

Fuseli saw that the Companion's chest was rising and falling rapidly, its enormous member now fully engorged and pointing toward him. The creature was visibly trembling.

"I have my doubts, madam," Yarlath said. "Somehow, my kind's path has never crossed with that of the Coleopteroids, as you call them. It may be that we are not aligned in such a way that travel between our universes is possible. At least, not *intentionally*. I'm afraid the best I can hope for in the near future is that my vanishing was witnessed by others in my household, and that efforts will be made to investigate, and track my whereabouts. Perhaps it might at least be possible for your kind to develop some method of sending a transmission to my people. An emergency beacon, if you will."

"Of course! I'm sure I'm speaking on behalf of my superiors when I tell you every effort will be made! We'll let them know about you straight away, and that might influence their decision as to whether we abandon this base for now, or make all our experimental equipment active again so we can resume our research immediately."

"For Chrissakes," Fuseli muttered to himself.

"Not to mention," Marceau said, "we have a sister research base on a planet called Jötunn, where the equipment is still intact."

"I suppose one doesn't know until one tries," said Yarlath. "In the meantime... ah, what do you suggest I do with myself? Do I remain standing in this burnt-out shell of a room like this, or am I permitted to move about freely?"

Fuseli spoke up before Marceau could answer. "Besides the terrorist, who's in custody, we have your other two iterations housed in comfortable rooms. One of them is a man from our world, who was acting as a test subject. He was in transit when the project was sabotaged and the rift was opened. The other iteration and all that came after were brought here accidentally, just like yourself. Anyway... what I suggest is, we give you and your Companion, here, your own rooms just like them. Due to the losses that were suffered in the explosion in this room, we have quarters available for you right now."

"Well, that is quite hospitable of you, Dr. Fuseli. I think now that we're all getting to know each other better, we're making some progress."

"Yes, I agree," Fuseli said. "So...like you said, we can't just stand around in here all day. Before we do anything else, let's show you to your rooms. We can give you both your own. After that, I'm sure Dr. Marceau here would be happy to take you on a tour of the entire base, personally."

Peripherally, Fuseli saw Tamati throw him a look of disbelief. He ignored it.

"Yes!" Marceau said enthusiastically. "I'd love to, Mr. Yarlath!"

"I should particularly like to meet my other iterations," Yarlath said. "I'm fascinated by the notion of being the first to meet iterations of myself of a type never before encountered by my kind." He tilted his head back a little, again as if listening to sounds only he could hear. "Alas, though, I now sense that one of the iterations I was previously aware of is no longer alive."

"What are you saying?" Fuseli said. "Which one of them is no longer alive?" He immediately thought of Rhan, so uncharacteristically afraid when he'd left her. Afraid enough to have harmed herself?

"It was the one you call a Coleopteroid, I would say."

"Impossible," the Liaison said. "Its wounds were not fatal. It is confined in a secure enclosure, with life support systems engaged."

"Be that as it may," said Yarlath, "it has died in the time that we have been speaking."

The Liaison pivoted to face Marceau and Fuseli. "I must go and investigate," it said. It then began floating toward the dome's exit.

"How sad," said Yarlath. "I wonder what happened?"

"Well, let's show you to your quarters," said Fuseli, "while we're waiting to hear what's going on. Will your Companion be okay walking through the base to get to his room? He's looking a little...distracted."

"As I keep telling you, Doctor," Yarlath said, "he is under my complete control."

-22-

Rhan knew she had been here before—though, not in *her* body.

She stood on a vast even surface, apparently of black metal, scored with what appeared to be sweeping geometric patterns that would only have properly revealed their shapes to her if seen from high above. These recessed grooves glowed inside with pulsing red light, to better define the patterns she somehow knew they formed.

On the horizon, either jagged mountains or the immense buildings of a great city rose toward a sky of greenish-black storm clouds, but these soaring mountains or structures were too distant to make out, and were made ghostly by a mist that glowed reddish from the patterns scored in the plain of black metal.

The air was humid, already damp with the threat of an approaching downpour. Within the boiling clouds she saw flickers of lightning, weirdly green in color, but she heard no thunder. Despite what appeared to be a gathering rainstorm, the air felt unnaturally heavy and still, with not even a breeze to stir her hair.

She was too much in awe to be terrified. Or, too terrified to even be aware of what she was feeling. All but paralyzed, she couldn't bring herself to shuffle around in a little circle to see what might lie behind her. More empty openness, or signs of civilization closer at hand? As it was, she had all she could do to tilt her head back and gaze straight up into the air, where she had sensed movement.

All at once, dozens—*hundreds*—of gigantic creatures were emerging from the dramatic clouds, through which no clear sky could be seen, only deeper depths of seething clouds. The creatures slipped out of the spaces between these mounded layers of clouds, their strangely incorporeal bodies trailing wisps of vapor.

The creatures were each as large as a house, she would guess, and they glowed red like the geometric patterns that were perhaps a message or signal to them. They reminded her somewhat of flowers blooming in time-lapse photography, only to close up and then bloom all over again. They also put her in mind of jellyfish, trailing squirming bundles of translucent red tentacles. These huge sky creatures struck her as being both mindless and frighteningly sentient at the same time...being either extremely primitive, or advanced beyond her comprehension.

Thousands now filled the air, and she stared up at them transfixed, statue-like—her heart having perhaps been stunned to motionlessness in her chest—as the sky creatures began to circle in a spiral up there, creating a vortex of their comingled bodies. A living funnel cloud that swirled directly above her, as if she herself were the eye of the growing storm.

The funnel cloud became an almost solid structure formed of their spinning, red-glowing bodies, so tightly amassed had they become. As if from many fragments, many cells, they were coming together to create a single entity. Many bodies into one body, that defied the limits of space and dimension.

From out of this monstrous funnel cloud, now blocking out all the rest of the stormy sky above her, a single creature detached itself from the rest. For a moment, it hung suspended at the very center of the vortex, directly above her. And then, as Rhan stood there gawking up at it, spellbound, the creature with its blooming body and writhing tendrils began to descend. Toward her. Descending lower...lower. Coming to her. Coming *for* her...

In her locked room at Base Gertrude, Rhan Luyen awoke from her vision with a scream, the spell broken.

She fought with her blanket, as if it were some ectoplasmic membrane that had settled over her and sought to absorb her. She finally threw it off and scrambled out of bed, backed herself up against a wall staring at her mattress in horror, afraid to again make herself vulnerable to such a nightmare.

Her door was unlocked, startling her, and it slid back to reveal Dr. Mann there, appearing concerned. The guard had let him in and stood just behind the medical chief.

"Rhan," said Mann, "are you all right? We heard you cry out."

"A dream...I think," she stammered. "A nightmare. Doctor, where is Robert? I mean, Dr. Fuseli?"

"Apparently he was called to some emergency in the dome. I was about to head there myself, but then Anthony over here was acting up and needed to be calmed down. And now, you too."

"Did he say he had a dream?"

"Yes, so it would seem. About a demon with red eyes." Mann watched her face carefully for signs of recognition. "This demon was trying to speak to him, he said. Did you by any chance dream something like that?"

"No...my dream was quiet. No voices this time. But there were these *things*... giant things in the sky..."

"*What?*" Mann said. "In the sky?"

Rhan continued, "And one of them wanted to join with me, I think." She looked away from Mann, toward a blank wall as she sought to remember. "Get into my head."

Mann and the guard exchanged glances, before Mann looked to Rhan again and started to speak. But just then, Captain Robert Fuseli entered that section of corridor...accompanied by a strange party. Mann turned in that direction, and Rhan heard him cry out, "Dear God!"

"What is it?" Rhan said, moving toward the open door.

"Close her door!" she heard Fuseli say out there in the hallway. "Quickly!"

Rhan had almost reached the doorway. "Robert!"

But the guard had lunged forward, and hit the control to close the door to her room. It slid shut in her face, and Rhan heard it lock.

-23-

The hallway guard had instinctively leveled his assault engine at the Companion, but Tamati gestured for him to hold off. Meanwhile, stricken by the sight of the two newcomers, Dr. Mann unconsciously backed himself against the corridor's wall between the doors to Anthony Nguyen's and Rhan Luyen's rooms, as Tamati stopped them in front of a room that had formerly been used by one of the test subjects killed in the dome's explosion.

Fuseli directed Tamati to open it. While this was happening, Mann exclaimed, "Dr. Marceau, what is this?"

Marceau started to answer, but Fuseli spoke over her. "This here is Mr. Yarlath—another of our alternates, and this strapping fellow is Mr. Yarlath's Companion, who came with him. It seems that where Mr. Yarlath comes from, they have the ability to influence the minds of their lesser selves. I'll tell you more soon enough. Mr. Yarlath, this is Dr. Russell Mann—Base Gertrude's medical chief."

Yarlath nodded politely. "Doctor."

"This is remarkable!" Mann said, looking between Yarlath and the towering, crimson-skinned Companion.

"Until we can figure out what steps to take next, in regard to how we might assist Mr. Yarlath, I wanted to find accommodations for them," Fuseli said. "We have a lot to discuss with them in the days ahead, and of course you'll want to be a part of that."

"Oh yes, of course, yes!" gushed Mann. "Oh, Mr. Yarlath, it's wonderful to meet you!"

"Likewise, I'm sure," Yarlath said, but his eyes had strayed to the closed door to Mann's left. "She's in there, isn't she? One of my iterations." Then his gaze shifted a bit, to the door on Mann's other side. "And the man is in there. He's the one who's native to this universe, isn't he?"

"That's correct," Fuseli said, "and I promise you'll meet them both soon enough. Let's just show you these rooms, first, so you're familiar with where you'll be staying. And of course, as such a highly advanced being, we'll permit you free range of the base once you're settled."

"Doctor Fuseli?" Marceau whispered, confused by his whole change in attitude.

As Fuseli stepped toward the open doorway, he made a point of catching Tamati's gaze. He flicked his eyes to the door controls meaningfully, then back to meet Tamati's eyes again. The security chief gave an almost imperceptible nod. Then, Fuseli stepped into the room, turned, and addressed Yarlath again.

"This will be where your Companion can stay. Have him come on in and have a look."

Without any word or visible cue from Yarlath, the Companion ducked its head and squeezed sideways into the tiny room. This was perhaps made somewhat easier by the fact that during their walk here, the creature had lost its monstrous erection.

"I know, it's very small," Fuseli said, shifting around the Companion to give it room to enter. "Maybe we can figure something else out for you later. At the very least—" he pointed at the narrow bed, to draw the creature's attention there "—we'll get another bed in here, and push them together to give you a little more room to sleep on."

Fuseli had managed to slip around behind the Companion, and while its attention was diverted toward the bed he leaped out through the open doorway. Even as the creature was whirling around to see what had happened, Tamati had already shot out his hand to hit the control to slide the door shut, and lock it. The other side of the door thudded with the Companion's impact, as it threw its bulk against the 3D-printed panel, but it held.

Again, with that uncanny speed he had demonstrated before, Yarlath pulled his knife from its hidden sheath and lunged forward, burying the red crystal blade in Fuseli's lower back.

However, before the Man from the Plane could twist the knife's handle, or drag its blade through Fuseli's flesh, Morris Tarragon stepped in and with all his strength behind it punched Yarlath in the side of his head. Yarlath managed to stay on his feet, but was spun around to face the hallway guard...who promptly struck Yarlath in the nose with the butt of his Drang. Yarlath collapsed to the floor, and Tamati was instantly on top of him, pinning him down. Tarragon knelt on the man's wrist and wrested the knife out of his hand.

Yarlath was still conscious, though dazed, and glared up at them. Inky black blood ran from his nostrils and smeared his teeth as he snarled at them, "Barbarians! How could I be so foolish as to let my guard down?"

Mann rushed to Fuseli, and took him by the arm. "We need to get you to the med unit!"

"No shit," said Fuseli, clamping a hand over the wound in his lower back on the right side. "I hope that missed my kidney."

"You motherfucker," Tarragon said, applying more weight to Yarlath's wrist.

"You'll be sorry," Yarlath hissed, a spittle of black blood flying from his lips. "Oh, you'll be sorry. Just wait until you open that door to deal with my friend."

"Let him try me," Tarragon said.

"Come on, come with me," Mann insisted.

"Hang on," Fuseli said. "Do we have a free room to lock this guy in?"

"That's it for the test subject rooms," said Tamati. "In the general barracks, yes..."

The Companion was now pounding on the locked door, and it seemed the entire hallway vibrated with each blow. And still, the creature made no vocalizations.

"Get Rhan out of her room," Fuseli winced, biting back the pain of his wound. "Then lock this bastard in there. I want Nguyen out of his room, too. I don't care where you put them, but make sure it's on the far side of the base. I don't want him exerting his influence on them, like he does with that monster."

"Will do, Captain," Tamati said. "But for God's sake, just go with Dr. Mann!"

The med unit's dog like quadruped robot had met them on the way, along with two of Mann's people, who loaded Fuseli onto a stretcher on the robot's back. Now, he lay face down and stripped naked on the medical unit's operating table while Mann saw to the deep knife wound in his back. There was the hissing of tissues being fused back together.

"At least," Mann muttered as he worked, "that blade didn't inject poison, or wasn't made of radioactive material or something."

"Don't give that guy ideas," said Fuseli, who was still conscious but feeling no pain in the area where Mann worked.

"When you get back home," Mann said, "you can have this finessed. As you've pointed out yourself, here one is forced to be more of a mechanic than an artist."

Marceau had opted to go with them, and stood outside the aseptic field watching Mann tend to the Colonial Forces officer. She said, "Why would you do that, Dr. Fuseli? *Why?* I thought we were coming to an understanding together."

"It would have all gone a lot better," Fuseli said, "and I might not be lying here right now, if you had left that creature inside the damn pod."

"Yarlath had Yukimi at knife point!"

"And *that* is why I 'did this'!" Fuseli said. "Let me tell you something about knives, Dr. Marceau. A person from a primitive culture might carry a knife because that's all he has for a weapon. Or because it's a tool he relies on. But a 'highly advanced being,' as this fucker wants us to believe he is, carrying a knife on him like that? Knives are an intimate way to kill...a *sexual* way. He carries that knife because he likes using it. You know he's done so before."

"We *don't* know that!"

"Look how quick he was to use it on Shimada and me! Did you not hear him describe his culture? Didn't you hear him say some of his people even slaughter and *eat* other sentient beings? Or is that okay with you...because he claims they only do that to their own alternate selves?"

"But...he said he doesn't do that, himself!"

"They hunt their alternates, too, some of them. Do you remember he said *that?*"

"So you're going to pass judgment on his entire race because of one conversation?"

"I'm not proposing we find his world and wipe his people out. I'm just proposing we never try to contact his people. That we never try to help him get back home. I think it's safe to say we don't ever want his civilization to know where we are. And I pity all those alternates of themselves they've already chanced upon in their travels."

"Well, what will we do with him, then?" asked Marceau. "And the Companion, which is basically just a poor animal under his thrall?"

"They'll have to remain as prisoners," Fuseli said simply. "I say they can't be trusted to ever be set free. But if you still want to interview Yarlath, Dr. Marceau, and see what you can learn from him in the future...by all means, do so. But believe me—he'll be on the other side of a protective barrier when you do it."

-24-

When Rhan emerged from her room, her eyes immediately locked onto the crimson eyes of the Man from the Plane.

"It's you," she said, horrified.

"Hello, my dear. I'm sorry to meet you in this state." Tamati and his security team carried handcuffs on them, and Yarlath's wrists were cuffed behind his back, so he wasn't free to wipe away the black blood still running thickly from his broken nose, and dripping onto the front of his beautiful silk top. In addition to the cuffs, Tamati pressed the muzzle of his pistol to the back of Yarlath's neck. "My, what a beautiful woman I would make, were it not for all that ghastly hair growing out of your head."

The hallway guard took Rhan by the arm and shifted her away from the threshold to her room, so Tamati could urge Yarlath inside. Tarragon pointed his own Scythe at Yarlath, and the guard kept his Drang ready, as Tamati holstered his handgun and undid the handcuffs.

"One more tricky move out of you," he said, "and these boys are going to shred you."

When the cuffs came off, Tamati quickly shoved Yarlath away from him, toward the bed. He'd seen how fast the Man from the Plane had got that knife into Fuseli. Then, he was jumping backwards through the doorway, and slamming the control to slide the door shut. But inside, Yarlath only turned to watch him calmly until the door had closed, rubbing at the wrist Tarragon had knelt on.

"Who is he?" Rhan asked breathlessly. "Is he the man who was telling me to come to the dome?"

"We'll tell you everything soon," Tarragon said. "You don't have anything in there he can use as a weapon, do you?"

"I came here with nothing, and I've been given nothing," she said. "But I did take a knife from the cafeteria."

"*What?* When? Where is it?"

Rhan reached under the top of her scrubs, and tucked in the waistband of her pants was the steak knife she'd spoken of. "I had it under the mattress," she admitted, "but I wanted it on me when I heard all the fuss going on out here."

"Jesus, you've had that all this time?" the guard blurted. No doubt he was thinking of the nearly hour and a half she and Fuseli had been alone in there.

Tarragon reached out and took the knife from her. "At least you're honest. Sometimes." He turned to Tamati. "Make a call...get two more guards down here, at least, to keep an eye on these doors. I don't care where you have to get them from."

"Will do." Tamati stepped away to make a call on his wrist comp.

"We're moving you and Nguyen away from here," Tarragon explained to Rhan. "That man can exert his control over his own alternates. That's what you're hearing in there." He pointed the steak knife at the booming door behind which the Companion raged. "One of his alternates, under his command."

Rhan stared at the quivering door, looking shellshocked.

"Guards on the way," Tamati said. "Okay, let's get Nguyen out of there, now, and I'll take them both across the base and find somewhere else to put them. I'm thinking the power plant, or the garage." He added for Rhan's understanding, "We're hoping he'll have less influence, the farther you are from him."

"Open him up," Tarragon said, having put the knife away in a pocket of his camos, and nodding toward the locked door of Anthony Nguyen's room.

The guard went ahead and punched in the code, and the door slid open, and in a flash Nguyen was on the man like a blood-crazed dog. While he grappled for the man's assault engine, trying to tear it from his hands, Nguyen got the guard's ear in his teeth. The man screamed, and together they crashed into the opposite wall.

"Oh my God! Oh my God!" Rhan cried.

Tarragon stepped in and brought the butt of his handgun down hard on the back of Nguyen's head. He had to do it twice, before Nguyen slumped to his knees. The guard slipped away from him along the wall, cursing and clamping a hand to his ear. Only the bottom half remained, the top portion still clamped in Nguyen's teeth.

As Tamati knelt down to use the same cuffs on Nguyen he had used on Yarlath, Nguyen spat out the torn portion of the guard's ear, looked up at Tarragon and said, "Barbarians. You'll be sorry...you just watch."

"I'd hit you again," said Tarragon, bending down to pick up the section of ear, "but Nguyen shouldn't have to be the one who suffers." He handed the piece of ear to the injured guard. "Here, go down to the med unit and give them that. They should be able to reattach it."

With that, he and Tamati hoisted Nguyen to his feet.

"Now you stay in here and rest," Mann said, as two of his assistants helped transfer Fuseli from the mobile operating table to a small, dark recovery room. "Whatever business you need to conduct, you do it from this bed for now."

"Where are those two injured guys...ah, Karlsson and Townsend?" Fuseli grunted, as he settled onto the bed.

"Recovering in their quarters now. Well, recovering as much as they can, until we can do more for them. I have their wrist comps transmitting their vital signs here, where we can monitor them."

"I need to call General Stroud at Port Haven, let him know about Yarlath and all that's just happened."

"And like I said, you can do that just fine from right in that bed." Mann took Fuseli's arm and held it while he punched in some entries on Fuseli's own wrist comp. "But first, let me get your device transmitting your vitals, too."

"Mann," Fuseli said, "will you go look in on the Coleopteroids? Yarlath claimed the prisoner is dead, and the Liaison went off to check on it. I haven't seen them again since."

"Oh? Really—dead? Yes...yes, of course, I'll go right now."

Just then, into the med unit came the guard from the hallway, reunited with Fuseli so soon, carrying the detached bit of ear in his hand, his face gummy with blood and twisted in pain. "Dr. Mann!" he groaned.

"Oh God, what now?"

Marceau said, "Dr. Mann, you stay here and take care of him... I'll go see to the Coleopteroids."

"Very well, very well." Mann went to take the injured guard by the arm to lead him to an examining table.

"Hey, private!" Fuseli called out from his adjacent room. "Please tell me Yarlath didn't break out!"

"It wasn't Yarlath," the guard groaned. "It was Nguyen."

To himself, Fuseli muttered, "God damn it. By now, that must be the same thing." Then he thought of Rhan...and wondered what invasion, what attempt at possession, she might be suffering just then, too.

-25-

"Dear God," said Olivia Marceau.

She was looking into the cylinder filled with softly-glowing orange fluid in which the saboteur had been imprisoned. Yet now, it no longer simply resembled a preserved biological specimen, but essentially *was* one. The Coleopteroid floating within was indeed dead, as was plain to see. It had plunged the pincers at the ends of its two tentacle-like upper limbs deeply into its own head on either side, successfully bursting through the chitin exoskeleton.

"Why do you think it did that?" Marceau asked the Liaison, who was now the only one of the team of Coleopteroid consultants left alive. The black-robed being stood beside her, also seeming to contemplate the grotesque corpse. "Do you think it did that so it wouldn't have to reveal the terrorist group it was working with?"

"I do not believe that to be the case," said the Liaison. "We were still not able to establish whether Technician 2 was acting on behalf of some political faction, or simply on its own. Now, we may never know. But, if Technician 2 were going to commit suicide rather than divulge information, it would no doubt have done so before this. Technician 2 did this only after the arrival of Yarlath. If Yarlath and Technician 2 truly are alternate selves, then I suspect Technician 2 was driven to do this by the connection Yarlath has with his alternates."

"You mean, Yarlath commanded it to kill itself?"

"No...I am saying, Technician 2 killed itself to avoid giving in to Yarlath's influence. It might not even have understood what it was experiencing, but was driven to a kind of madness." The Liaison pivoted to look down at Marceau directly. "Before you came, Dr. Marceau, I was in conversation with my superiors.

A new team of my people will be teleporting from our world to our base on Earth, and from there departing immediately aboard an Earth Colonies vessel. I am to remain here to meet with them and continue in my role."

"Oh, that's great."

"However, our priorities have somewhat changed, Doctor," said the Liaison. "We will continue to assist your people in developing your own teleportation technology, but only when we feel it is safe to resume. Before that, this new team will be primarily focused on identifying the anomalous rift, if it still remains open after our having shut down the prototype pod and our associated navigation system. If the rift is found to still exist, the new team must find a means of closing it before any further experiments can continue."

"I see. Well...of course, that makes sense."

"If in the end the rift can not be closed, if it is not closed already, then my superiors advise that Base Gertrude should be evacuated and destroyed, and another base erected on another planet or moon. In fact, if there is a possibility that, by connection, the base on Jötunn also needs to be destroyed to ensure the rift is no longer active, then that course of action might be necessary, as well."

"Oh no!" Marceau said. "Oh God, I hope it doesn't come to that! If we had to start all over again from scratch, on two different planets..."

"I understand your concern, Doctor, and I share it. We must do our best to see that it does not come to that. But you see, the reason why we might need to take such drastic action is quite clear. We cannot allow Yarlath's kind—these people from the Plane, as he calls his world—to track him here, to this universe, and possibly follow after him."

"What are you saying? You mean you share Dr. Fuseli's belief...that Yarlath's whole race is dangerous?"

"I do, doctor. And having heard my report, so do my superiors. The culture Yarlath describes is that of conquerors, who exploit those other races they deem inferior to their own. His contempt even for my people—who like his, have already mastered interplanetary and extradimensional teleportation—was quite plain to me. My superiors feel Yarlath's kind pose too great of a threat for us to risk interaction with."

"Then, what will we do with him, if not try to help him contact his people and get him back home?"

"He must be forever kept a prisoner, Doctor. I am sure your own government will agree, when they confer with mine—which will be happening even as we speak. In fact," the Liaison went on, "our recommendation to the Earth Colonies government will be that Yarlath should be eliminated."

"Eliminated," Marceau echoed, turning her gaze back to the dead Technician 2 in its transparent coffin.

Rhan was again at the Plane.

Though still standing upon that seemingly endless surface of black metal, scored with enigmatic patterns of pulsing red light, this time she was nearer to what she'd thought before might have been mountains on the horizon. They were, as she had also considered, great buildings after all: a city of black metal. The structures were of varied height and size, but dominating them was a black metal pyramid, greater still than all the rest, soaring against the sky of boiling greenish-black storm clouds, that flashed here and there with discharges of vivid green lightning.

The city was still rather misted with distance, even as it loomed in front of her so colossally, but she was grateful not to see it more clearly. It was too monstrous for her mind to take in. Especially since above the city hung what looked from here like a blizzard of red snow. Or some sort of restless, red-glowing pollen. Yet, she knew what those seemingly tiny particles actually were. Each and every swarming red speck out there was one of those flower-like, tentacled sky creatures.

"Impressive, isn't it?" purred a seductive voice at her neck.

Rhan whirled around, and there stood Yarlath, smiling at her calmly, handsome and unbloodied.

"Are we really here?" she asked him, in a dazed voice as if talking in her sleep. "You brought me to your world?"

"I haven't...though I would like to. And perhaps, if my people can find me and rescue me from those who have captured the both of us—you and I—I will bring you to this place to live with me. And what a life we would live, eh, Rhan? We could be mated...two expressions of the same being. What joining between two people could ever be more intimate? More marvelous?"

"No. Now you sound like Nguyen."

"That crude being? He could never hope to join with you as I can. But again, no, I didn't bring you to my world...I have merely entered your mind. As best I can under these conditions, at least. This is simply a memory, an *awareness*, of the Plane that I am sharing with you."

"I don't want to go there," she told him.

"My kind didn't want to in the beginning, either—the first of us who were brought to the Plane. But now that we are born there, we realize how fortunate we are, to serve as what we call the First Vessels."

"The...*First* Vessels?"

"All the lesser iterations we encounter and master are simply extensions of these primary vehicles. I may not have made my situation entirely clear to the people who captured me. You see, just as my Companion is controlled by me, yet at the same time retains what little he has of his individual mind, so too do I house another consciousness. The *highest* self." With that, Yarlath tilted back his head to stare straight upward. Rhan followed his gaze...and gasped with shock.

This time, the sky above her was empty of the swarming sky creatures, except for this solitary specimen. Huge, translucent, and perhaps not truly corporeal, it floated directly above Yarlath's head. And now, finally, Rhan realized that the very end of one of its trailing tendrils—which grew more faint and hard to discern the farther they were from the creature's body—was rooted in the top of Yarlath's hairless skull. The creature hung above him, tethered to him, like a parachute caught in a wind she couldn't feel, billowing with rhythmic movement and prevented from collapsing to earth.

"You see, they are the true Dwellers of the Plane. They didn't colonize the Plane; they brought *us*, the First Vessels, here to colonize it...so that they might have physical vehicles to occupy. We give them hands. We give them sensation."

"You're just a puppet!" Rhan exclaimed, trying to fight her way out of her drowsy state.

"Now, now, don't be insulting," said Yarlath. "It is a privilege to serve as the First Vessels of the Dwellers. They act through us, even as we retain our foundation minds. It is the best of both worlds—a coming together of two worlds, or states of being. A symbiotic relationship. We provide the Dwellers the physical sensation they desire, the ability to act in the material worlds that beings like you and I occupy, and in turn they provide my kind with abilities we would otherwise not possess. My ability to control the Companion, for instance, and to speak with you now inside your head...do you think I could do those things on my own, without this bond to my higher self? Why, its power is so great that I am conjoined with it even now...while I am here in the universe of these Earth people, but my higher self remains back there on the Plane."

"While you're so separated like that, you should try to break the connection!"

Yarlath cocked his head quizzically. "My dear...*why would I want to?*"

"You've been a puppet so long, you don't even know you are one! You and all your people are enslaved!"

Yarlath wagged his head sadly. "You are just a child, so I will forgive your disrespectful words."

"This is why your kind think they can just kill your other selves...hunt them... eat them! You don't value their lives because you're seeing them through the eyes of that...*monster.*" Rhan pointed up into the sky, at the Dweller that hung there so enormous and silent. As if it were only listening to Yarlath speak...instead of speaking through him.

Yarlath grinned, and joked, "It *has* no eyes." Then he said, "Despite your ignorant insults, I admire your strength. That insect-creature in its tank was driven to such madness that it killed itself, and that man Anthony Nguyen is little better, raging like a lunatic. But you, my dear, are holding up quite well...which is why I can see us joining in the future. Hopefully on the Plane, but if not, then in this universe...someplace where they can not imprison me again. But first, I must free myself from these humans. Won't you help me, Rhan? In any way you can, so that we can be together?"

"I won't help you!" Rhan growled. She was getting clear, coming awake.

"You are trapped in their world the same as I am! Can you not see how unfair that is, and how unjustly these savages treat the two of us? We must *both* be free!"

"They could help both of us, if we let them! It's an accident that we're here!"

"You are a fool if you believe you will ever live as anything other than a specimen, a curiosity, if you do not let me help you. But I need your help, as well."

"No!" Rhan shouted. "I won't help you!" She stabbed her finger toward the Dweller, its tendrils stirring as if in a lazy ocean current. That is, those tendrils that weren't anchored in Yarlath's brain. She repeated, "*I won't help you!*"

-26-

"Rhan!" Fuseli said, clamping a hand on her shoulder.

The contact startled her awake, and she looked up at him in a wild-eyed shock of disorientation. Fuseli thought there was even terror in the mix. She recoiled from him and backed herself up against the wall, until she seemed to finally realize who it was she was facing and visibly became less tense.

"You were saying, 'I won't help you,'" Fuseli said.

"I wasn't dreaming!"

"I didn't say you were."

"He was in my head—Yarlath!"

He wasn't surprised to hear this, and had even expected it. It was the reason he had left the medical unit and walked all the way here to check on her, despite Dr. Mann's excited protests when the medical chief realized his patient was sneaking out on him when his back was turned. Mann had chased him out into the hallway, calling after him, but Fuseli had ignored him and kept going. On the way to the far side of Base Gertrude, Fuseli had got General Stroud on his wrist comp, to fill him in on all that was happening with this latest alien being to have been delivered at the research site, courtesy of the unidentified anomaly they'd created.

It turned out that Stroud had already been informed of the basics, due to the Liaison having contacted its Coleopteroid superiors, and they in turn having expressed their concerns to the government of the Earth Colonies network. Stroud had also been notified of Fuseli's potentially fatal wounding, but that he was being treated for it. His injury was the reason Stroud had refrained from contacting Fuseli personally, until he was well enough to report in.

Fuseli had had to ask a Colonial Forcer he'd chanced upon, along the way, exactly where Rhan and Nguyen had been moved to. He'd been told Anthony Nguyen had been locked in a storage room adjacent to the garage, with two guards placed outside. Rhan had been secured inside another storage room, this one attached to the power plant, again with two guards outside its door—one of these being Private Amaka Sunday, who had nodded to Fuseli in greeting as she saw him approach. Before asking Amaka to unlock the door for him, he'd asked her how Rhan was doing. Amaka replied that Rhan hadn't been causing any trouble in there and had gone inside willingly—unlike Nguyen, she pointed out, who'd had to be dragged into his makeshift cell—but she said she'd heard Rhan talking to herself in there. And when the door had been opened, Fuseli had heard that for himself...finding Rhan agitated and ranting, seemingly experiencing a nightmare as she lay on an improvised bed of packing foam on the storage room's floor.

Fuseli had knelt down beside her, on the edge on the stacked foam sheets, and now he asked, "Rhan...what's your daughter's name?"

Her face twisted in confusion. "*What?* Why are you asking me this now, Robert? Her name is Fhuy."

Fuseli nodded, satisfied. Even her saying his name, *Robert,* had relived him. Yarlath wouldn't have called him that.

"You're afraid he's possessed me," she said in realization.

"Just being careful," Fuseli said. "Tell me what you experienced. Tell me everything."

"You tell me everything, too," she said, leaning toward him urgently then and putting a hand on his arm as she came fully alert. "The soldiers told me he stabbed you, Robert!"

"Eh, I've had worse," Fuseli said, smiling. Her hand holding his arm and the concern in her dark eyes were better medicine than Mann had provided.

For the second time since Fuseli had arrived at Base Gertrude, he and Tarragon and the heads of the base's various departments gathered in the meeting room, on this occasion with General Stroud participating via a large holographic screen. Olivia Marceau, Russell Mann, Yukimi Shimada taking over for the late Santosh Chawla, security chief Rhys Tamati, and the Coleopteroid Liaison were all in attendance.

"So this is what it is," Stroud started out, his words coming on a heavy sigh. "The Earth Colonies government has been in discussions with that of the Coleopteroids, who have been kept apprised of events thanks to their Liaison. As the Liaison has already told Dr. Marceau, the Coleopteroids will be sending a new team there, and they should arrive at Titania in two weeks. Before the dome lab can be fully restored and teleportation research resume, the new team's priority will be to isolate the anomaly that caused the teleportation of extradimensional beings into our universe—if that anomaly still exists. If it was *not* negated by the actions you people took there, the new team will undertake efforts to do so, using their own preexistent technology."

Marceau had already told Fuseli that this was the Coleopteroids' planned course of action, as revealed to her by the Liaison, so he waited for the rest...the part that concerned him, and what he was to do personally.

"Dr. Marceau," the Colonial Forces general instructed, "you and your staff of researchers will remain, doing what restoration to the dome lab you can, pending the arrival of the new Coleopteroid team."

"Oh, thank goodness," she gushed, smiling over at Dr. Mann.

"Excellent," said Mann.

"Your continued commitment to this important project is appreciated," said Stroud mechanically, as if such a statement was required of him. "However, as we still can't be sure that the anomaly is no longer active—despite your assurances that no further alien beings have manifested there since this Yarlath person—we believe it's prudent to remove the test subject Anthony Nguyen and all his alternate selves, living and dead, from Base Gertrude...in case their presence there might still interact with the anomaly. We don't understand its mechanics, but it was clearly drawing in Nguyen's parallel selves from other universes and delivering them to his approximate location, so it seems a good idea to remove him from that site."

"I understand," said Marceau.

"Unfortunate, though," said Mann. "I would have liked to have studied the alternates more."

"Oh, rest assured they'll be studied elsewhere," said Stroud. "We're going to have them moved first to Port Urano, in orbit around Uranus, just to get them out of there as soon as possible. A military destroyer will be sent to Port Urano to gather them all up and take them back here to Port Haven. We're closer to you here than you are to Earth, and the less time those specimens are in transit the better."

"Understood," said Mann.

Stroud switched his attention to Fuseli. "Bob, given that you were seriously wounded and your job at Base Gertrude was fulfilled—that being, to investigate the appearance of the first extradimensional, Rhan Luyen—I want you to come home. You are to accompany the specimens to Port Urano. Morris, of course, will come with you."

Fuseli said, "Yes sir...thank you. I agree that's for the best." Not only did he want to see to it that Rhan was treated well, and to comfort her with his presence, but he wanted to personally make sure Yarlath and his Companion were secured.

"You'll be leaving for Port Urano aboard two ships," Stroud resumed. "You and Morris, four more security people, Anthony Nguyen, Rhan Luyen, Yarlath, and that...Companion of his will travel in the patrol craft the Khopesh, piloted by Lieutenant Dalia Halabi and Lieutenant Christopher Rix."

"Got it," said Fuseli. Stroud knew that would be his preferred arrangement.

Stroud continued, "Aboard a second patrol craft will be two of Base Gertrude's staff pilots, four more security people, and all the dead specimens."

Fuseli ticked off a list in his head. The dead would include the blue-skinned stranger, who had shot and killed Corporal Hoxha. There was the white-armored Coleopteroid-like being that had killed Chawla. The being with a face that reminded him of a tapeworm, found already dead outside, and the blob-like thing they had taken for an aquatic creature, found already dead inside the base. The tiny creature that had savaged the maintenance tech Karlsson, and finally Technician 2.

"Sir," Fuseli cut in, "couldn't the Khopesh accommodate all those specimens in its cargo hold?"

"It could, Bob, and I know it's not far to Port Urano, but I'd prefer to have two military craft go forth instead of just one, in the event of pirates. Which threat, incidentally, was why my superiors nixed the idea of abandoning Base Gertrude altogether, or at least until the project could be restarted. They were afraid pirates might be watching, and move in to take over the place."

"Makes sense."

"So it's best if the ship with the dead specimens serves as your escort."

"Not to mention," Fuseli said, "if pirates did attack, or something else went wrong and the Khopesh was destroyed, you'd at least still have a ship full of valuable dead specimens, so it wouldn't be a total loss. Better than putting all your eggs in one basket."

"Bob," Stroud said, "come on, now. Neither ship is close to being expendable."

"Since the dead specimens will be in the hold and you'll have room on the second ship," Fuseli said, "I want to take three injured people back to Port Haven with us. I promised them I'd see to their injuries myself. A tech, Oskar Karlsson, and a C-Forcer, Private Townsend, plus another Forcer who had his ear bitten off."

"Jesus. Yes, of course, that's fine," Stroud said. "But will they be okay enough to ride on the other ship without you beside them?"

"Thanks. Yeah, they'll be okay until we get to Port Urano. So when do you want us to head out, then?"

"As soon as you can, Bob," said Stroud. "As in, immediately."

-27-

An anxious Dr. Mann accompanied Fuseli, Tarragon, Tamati, and two Colonial

Forces grunts to the barracks area—where four guards were already stationed outside the rooms containing Yarlath and his Companion.

"But Dr. Fuseli," Mann was protesting, "we don't understand Yarlath's system enough to know if that drug will even have an effect on him...or whether it might kill him instead of only putting him to sleep!"

"Oh well," said Fuseli. "They still want dead specimens, don't they?"

"Is that your attitude toward Rhan, as well?"

Fuseli came to a quick stop, forcing the others to follow suit. His eyes might have burned holes straight through the back of Mann's head. "Rhan isn't a dangerous psychopath," he said. Then he thought of her daughter Fhuy...and Rhan's boyfriend. He hadn't shared her confession with anyone yet but Tarragon, though he knew he'd have to admit it to Stroud eventually. "Do you think I mean to kill him intentionally, and write it off as an accident?"

"Of course not, but—"

"It's a risk we have to take."

"And simply cuffing his wrists and ankles won't do?"

"Oh, he'll find himself wearing those, when he wakes up aboard the Khopesh."

"Captain," Tamati spoke up. He'd been uncomfortably silent while they'd been on their way here. "The Companion...wouldn't it be safer just to shoot the thing? Give them *that* as a dead specimen? I'm afraid the drug won't work on it quickly enough to stop it from doing some damage."

"I've taken its size into consideration and increased the dosage," Fuseli said. In Tarragon's hands was a spear-like instrument they'd improvised using a long, rigid shaft they'd had one of the base's engineers 3D print for them. Inserted into this tube's open end was a syringe filled with the powerful, fast-acting sedative they discussed. In case the syringe was broken or dislodged, or the dosage proved insufficient, Tarragon had several more filled syringes in a pocket of his camos to fit into the spear. He had been designated as the one to jab the proto-human when the door to its room was opened. The plan was to then quickly secure the door again until the drug took effect and the Companion was immobilized. Then, they'd shackle it. They'd had the same engineer 3D print cuffs large enough to accommodate the Companion's wrists and ankles, too...first having lent him regular restraints to use as his models. They could only hope the end results would be strong enough to hold the thing. Fuseli said, "Killing it isn't off the table, though, if it comes to that. But first—Yarlath."

They approached Rhan's former room, where Fuseli had lain with her. Remembering this, he was unsettled by the awareness that they were two versions of the same being, but it was still too much for him to wrap his head around. Could they really both be mere limbs of a single cosmic consciousness—or soul, if one were religious—that bristled with infinite such limbs?

Fuseli nodded to Tamati, who went forward to punch in the code to unlock the door. Meanwhile, six Colonial Forcers leveled their Drangs from their hips, gripping them two-fisted and ready to unleash a firestorm.

The door slid back, and Yarlath stood there near the foot of the narrow bed smiling at them cordially, despite the black blood marring the front of his top from his swollen, broken nose. He had apparently heard them talking just outside, and spread his arms out as if offering himself to them. When he spoke, as always, the words they heard and the movement of his lips didn't correspond. "Are you here to execute me, then, Dr. Fuseli?"

"Only if you want it that way," said Fuseli, uncapping the syringe he held. Since talking with Rhan about her visions, he saw Yarlath now through new eyes—not knowing how much he was speaking with the man physically in front of him, and how much he might truly be conversing with one of the mysterious extradimensional Dwellers that had apparently enslaved Yarlath's race generations ago.

"How is your wound, by the way?" Yarlath asked him. "You look well enough. My kind possess an organ in our lower right side that performs a critical function. Had you been one of my people, that wound would have proved instantly fatal."

To Fuseli, the Man from the Plane sounded as though he had to preserve his pride, by making excuses for not having succeeded in killing him. "Thanks," Fuseli said, entering the room. "I'll make a mental note of that, in case I do need to kill you."

"What I mean to say is, we don't understand each other's makeup sufficiently well." Yarlath nodded at the syringe in Fuseli's hand. "How do you know that won't kill me? Are you willing to risk it...and lose all the knowledge I might impart to you, about my people? About our technology...the many discoveries we've made in our travels?"

"Yes," said Fuseli. "I am. Roll up your sleeve and hold out your arm. Your choice of arms. You make one funny move and you'll be turned to confetti."

"Confetti?"

"Shredded paper."

Yarlath did as he was told, baring the pure white skin of his left arm and then extending it in front of him. Fuseli moved in with the syringe, while on either side of him, a Colonial Forcer aimed their assault engine directly at Yarlath's face.

Fuseli injected him successfully, then quickly backed off. He knew how much quicker Yarlath could be. "You might want to sit down on the bed. This will hit you fast."

"I suppose I should." Yarlath seated himself on the end of his cot-like bed, rolling down again the sleeve of his silvery top. "You must be moving me somewhere."

"It's a surprise," Fuseli said.

"I see. Well, I rather like surprises."

Mann pushed in behind Fuseli. "How are you feeling, Mr. Yarlath?"

"Actually, I am feeling drowsy already, Dr. Mann. Thank you for asking."

"We don't want to hurt you, you know," Mann said. "If you cooperate, my people might still help you yet."

"Will they, now?" said Yarlath.

Fuseli put away the empty syringe, watching his prisoner-turned-patient critically. Mann watched him avidly, too, and said, "You should let me put a wrist comp on him, so we can monitor his vital signs."

"Right now, we wouldn't know how to interpret the readings," said Fuseli, "and we don't have time to scan him and calibrate one. You just keep back."

"Oh my," said Yarlath, who then gave a hearty yawn. "Yes...this is taking effect rapidly, isn't it? Do you mind if I lie down?"

"I insist," said Fuseli.

Yarlath stretched out full-length on his bed, stiffly, with his arms at his sides. "Well, I do hope I'll wake up to see your faces again, gentlemen."

"Yeah," Fuseli said. "See you on the other side."

Yarlath closed his eyes, and they watched him for a time. The rising and falling of his chest became slower and deeper, but it didn't come to a halt. Finally, Fuseli drew his sidearm, walked over to Yarlath and pressed the handgun's muzzle to Yarlath's head.

"Doctor, no!" Mann started toward him.

"Keep back, I said!" Fuseli nodded to Tamati. "Okay, then...cuff him."

"Aw, fuck this," said Morris Tarragon, braced in front of the door with his lance held out in front of him.

Fuseli had his Scythe in one hand, and a second syringe ready in the other. Tamati had his pistol drawn, too, as he reached out to the door's control keys. Around them, the six Colonial Forcers with their Drangs were poised for action.

"Here we go, kids," Fuseli said. "If we have to light him up, just be sure Lieutenant Tarragon isn't in your line of fire." Then, he gave a nod to Tamati, who nodded back and punched the code to unlock the door.

The panel slid back halfway...then jammed in its track. It had become buckled by all the Companion's pounding against it.

"Damn it," Tarragon growled. "Going in!" He squeezed in through what opening he had.

"Go, go, go!" Fuseli shouted.

Two of the C-Forcers slipped in after Tarragon, and then he followed after himself. He couldn't see past the bodies of those in front of him yet, but so far he hadn't heard any gunfire.

Then, he was through, and the only thing to jump in his face was the room's smell. There was a heavy animal musk, but it was overwritten with the smell of excrement—both fresh and caked—that had been hurled against all four walls and manually smeared. The room hadn't contained much that could be broken or destroyed, but what could be had been. The little flip-down desk: torn out of the wall. Its chair: smashed. The wall screen ripped out, and the bed frame broken into pieces. It appeared the Companion had planned to use one long portion of the smashed bed frame as a spear of its own, the way it leaned in a corner.

But the Companion itself lay curled on its side on the floor, half on the inadequate mattress and half off, as if peacefully asleep despite their noisy entrance. Tarragon stood over it, his lance ready to thrust. He looked up at Fuseli questioningly.

"I don't think it's dead...but I don't think it's only asleep," he said.

Fuseli said, "When we put Yarlath under, it looks like the Companion lost consciousness, too. Let's not take chances, though." Fuseli himself went over to the red-skinned, ape-like giant with its pattern of strange black tattoos...which made him to recall the eerie sky creatures Rhan had described to him from her visions. *The Dwellers of the Plane*, she'd said. As two more soldiers crowded into the room behind him, and the last two worked together to shove the door panel open all the way, Fuseli knelt down beside the Companion and injected it with the syringe he carried. The massive body went on breathing deeply without even flinching.

"Okay," he said, looking up at the others. "Get this thing shackled up."

The drugged bodies of Yarlath (carried on a stretcher by the dog-like med robot) and the Companion (lashed onto a shipping pallet carried by a warehouse forklift robot) were borne away toward the central tram hub, accompanied by Mann and Tamati. Fuseli had ordered Mann to inject them again if either began to wake up, and Tamati was there to make sure Mann followed through. The six C-Forcers went with them.

Then, Fuseli and Tarragon crossed the base to collect the Khopesh's last two passengers: Anthony Nguyen and Rhan Luyen.

Outside the power plant storage room, Amaka Sunday and another guard stood ready as Fuseli prepared to open the door. Ahead of time, Tamati had called them on their wrist comps to let them know Fuseli was coming for Rhan, and he'd told these two that they would be among the four security grunts riding aboard the Khopesh to Port Urano.

Fuseli let himself into the storage room, where Rhan lay on her side on the stacked layers of foam that served as her bed. She wasn't unconscious, however, but sprang right to her feet like a wary animal ready to flee, though there was nowhere to flee to. Fuseli smiled to reassure her.

"We're taking you out of here, Rhan," he explained. "Don't worry, I'll be going with you. I'll tell you everything later, but for now we need to get to the ship. Just think: your first time riding in a spaceship."

"That's nothing," she said dryly. "I've already teleported between dimensions."

Fuseli took her by the arm gently and guided her out of the room. "Now," he told her, "lastly we collect the guy who caused us all these headaches. Tony Nguyen."

"Oh?" Rhan said, as she started walking beside him. "So am I a headache, then?"

Fuseli chuckled. "Well, that but so much more."

When the door of the garage storage room whisked open, Anthony Nguyen also lay on his improvised bed—most likely out of boredom—and again, for a moment Fuseli wondered if he were unconscious, but Nguyen too scrambled to his feet.

"What's going on?" he asked, as Tarragon and two C-Forcers came into the room, followed by Fuseli with a syringe ready.

"You look more like yourself at the moment, Tony," Fuseli said. "How are you feeling?"

"I'm feeling a little beat up, to be honest." He rubbed the back of his head, then warily noticed the syringe. "So what's up?"

"We're taking you to another base," Fuseli explained. "Port Urano. We'll all wait there together until a military ship can meet us and take us to Port Haven."

Tarragon moved in to cuff Nguyen's hands in front of him, and Nguyen held out his arms for the big security officer cooperatively. They left his ankles unshackled, and Fuseli pocketed the syringe as unneeded.

"Sounds good to me," Nguyen said. "After all the crazy shit here, I'll almost be happy to get back to prison. Then again," he added, looking past Fuseli to throw a wink at Rhan, "I'll miss seeing you, beautiful."

Rhan only groaned.

PART FIVE:

The Tram

-1-

The ship that would carry the dead specimens, the injured base staff, and escort the Khopesh was an identical military patrol craft named the F.C.S. Assegai, and a tram had already departed from the central hub carrying its passengers both living and dead, to where waiting Base Gertrude crewmembers would load up the Assegai at launch pad 2-B. Meanwhile, the Khopesh would lift off from pad B of the third launch station, where it had remained ever since delivering Fuseli and Tarragon to Titania.

Dr. Marceau, Dr. Mann, Lieutenant Tamati, and the Coleopteroid Liaison had assembled in the tram hub station to see off Fuseli and the rest. While Fuseli waited for base crew to load the unconscious Yarlath and Companion onto the tram they'd be taking out to Launch Station 3, they exchanged their goodbyes. Rhan stood beside him, unshackled, while Nguyen stood nearby handcuffed but uncomplaining.

"Well, Dr. Marceau," Fuseli said, "best of luck to you on continuing your project. I hope it goes more smoothly henceforth. Sorry if I was successful in seeing that your exciting interdimensional portal got shut down."

"I suppose I'll have to content myself with my original line of research, Dr. Fuseli," she said.

"But please," Mann said, "do take care of those three very important individuals, Dr. Fuseli. There is so much to learn from them."

"I will," Fuseli assured him. He was already determined to accompany Rhan Luyen wherever they ended up sending her, and was confident General Stroud would see to it that he was indeed assigned according to his request. He had reassured Rhan of his intentions.

Tamati stepped forward to salute Fuseli, and then shake his hand. "Captain, it was an honor serving under your command. If there was any real justice, with your accomplishments you'd have been promoted to colonel a long time ago, but I know the politics involved."

Fuseli grinned. "Hell, I might be Surgeon General by now if I just stopped butting heads with people." He clapped Tamati on the shoulder. "You're a good man, Rhys. Keep these people safe."

"Will do, sir."

Fuseli turned to the Liaison. The neat bullet hole in its cheek had closed up by now, without leaving a scar. Its torn ear, too, had regenerated without him having noticed until just now. He said, "Thank you for helping us deal with these complex problems here...and again, I'm sorry for the loss of your team. Best of luck with the next one. Hopefully, there'll be no saboteurs among them."

"The next team is being scrutinized very carefully, Dr. Fuseli," the Liaison replied. "My people express their deepest regrets for the loss of life brought about by Technician 2's actions. We only hope our continued assistance to your people can make up for this tragedy. Our investigation into Technician 2's possible involvement in a political faction will continue, I assure you."

Fuseli wasn't entirely sure the full results of that investigation would be shared with the Earth Colonies government, but he thanked the Liaison again, anyway.

Marceau and Mann said their goodbyes to Rhan, and thanked Nguyen for having participated in Base Gertrude's research...and then it was time for them to board the tram, too, and ride it out to Launch Station 3 and the waiting Earth Colonies Ship Khopesh.

Since the passenger tram was so small, when there was cargo to haul between the base and the distant launch stations one or more freight cars could be linked to the main car. That was the case now, with the seven-foot Companion, strapped onto a shipping pallet that would be stowed in a closed-off freight car. They managed to get one of the helmets for venturing outside the base onto its head, after first removing some of the cushioning inside meant for a comfortable fit, and they secured the helmet's edges with a special tape to keep the air inside the helmet—provided by the cartridge of compressed air inserted into its back—secure. If the Companion woke up between the base and the Khopesh and became agitated about the helmet, Fuseli said, hopefully the straps lashing it in place and the manacles on wrists and ankles would hold it.

"What if it did break free in there, sir?" Amaka asked him.

"Then we leave it in that box until its air runs out," he said, "and the scientists on Port Haven get another dead specimen."

With cargo and passengers in place, the tram departed from Base Gertrude proper, whispering along its repulsor track toward Launch Station 3 with its four individual launch pads. Pilot Halabi and copilot Rix had already gone on ahead to get the Khopesh prepped, along with some techs to doublecheck systems and a few extra pairs of hands who would help transfer the Companion into the patrol craft's hold, once this tram got there.

Given Yarlath's powers and how he had tried to influence Rhan to join forces with him, Fuseli still couldn't allow himself to trust her so completely that he sat beside her on the tram—where she had easy access to his holstered handgun—so he stood over her in the cramped aisle, holding an overhead rail as if they rode beneath some city on Earth instead of across the frozen wasteland of Titania. She had turned her face to the tram's windows, to watch that icy barrenness pass by through the transparent, segmented tube that enclosed the tram's repulsor tracks. She was quiet, seemed lost in thought, or perhaps only contemplated the gargantuan crescent moon that was actually the planet Uranus, in anticipation of her first flight into space.

Fuseli switched his attention to Yarlath, reclined in his seat with his head back and eyes shut, his cuffed hands resting in his lap. They had decided to plunk him into a seat instead of remaining on his stretcher, simply out of practicality. About this, watching Yarlath warily also, Amaka spoke to Fuseli again.

"Maybe it would have been better to bring him and the space chimp to Port Urano on Base Gertrude's medevac, Captain?"

"That medevacs isn't a military ship," Tarragon said gruffly, having overheard her. "It doesn't have guns...which is no good out here if pirates spot us."

"Got it, sir. Sorry to question, sir."

Fuseli smiled at her sympathetically, and then looked over at Anthony Nguyen. Also with his hands cuffed in his lap, Nguyen gazed out the windows on the other side of the tram, across the floor of the colossal crater named Gertrude—at a frozen landscape that seemed to offer open, boundless freedom but actually only the freedom of instant death.

Fuseli looked down at Rhan again. A sudden sense of alarm filled him, when he saw her face reflected in the window and realized her eyes were closed, as if she had fallen asleep. Asleep so quickly? True, none of them had slept much or slept well lately—Fuseli relying on stimulant pills, and Tarragon apparently on sheer willpower—but they hadn't even left the base half a minute ago. He let go of the rail to bend down over her more closely.

"Rhan," he said, putting a hand on her arm.

Fuseli dreaded seeing her eyes open calmly...seeing her turn to him with an eerily pleasant smile and say, "I'm quite all right, I assure you...*Dr. Fuseli.*"

Instead, Rhan jolted awake and for a second looked panicky, until she recognized the face above her own. "Are we there, Robert?"

"We only just started. You're pretty tired, huh?"

"I think I was there again...on the Plane," she whispered, throwing a nervous glance over at Yarlath. "I didn't see *him* there, but I saw that city in the distance... that pyramid...and those jellyfish-things, all floating above it."

"Did you feel like you were really there again, or only having a nightmare about what happened before?"

"I honestly don't know."

Fuseli straightened, looked toward Yarlath again, and then crossed over to him. From what he could tell, Yarlath truly appeared to be unconscious, thanks to the drug they'd administered, but how could he be positive? True, as Mann had said, a properly calibrated wrist comp could have provided him with readings on Yarlath's system and state of consciousness, but the Man from the Plane hadn't exactly given them much of an opportunity to run a proper series of mapping scans on his entire body, by which to do such calibrations.

He reached out then, applied the ball of his thumb to Yarlath's broken nose, and applied pressure. He put real weight behind it.

Neither Yarlath's eyelids nor any other muscle in his face so much as twitched. The alien went on breathing peacefully, with something almost like a tiny smile on his full-lipped mouth...which reminded Fuseli disturbingly of Rhan's own.

"Captain!" he heard Tarragon shout then...and that wasn't good, because Lieutenant Morris Tarragon wasn't given to cries of surprise.

More cries of surprise, and fear, from others riding in the tram soon followed it.

-2-

It was Fuseli's first time seeing the crab being, except in the video Tarragon had showed him from his patrol in the rover.

With the odd, slow-motion way the giant creature scrambled toward them across the flat expanse of icy rock, it appeared to be moving underwater, though that actually had to do with Titania's low gravity. Again, Fuseli was reminded of a long-legged Japanese spider crab, but covered in thick gray fur, and with about a dozen bony tubes sprouting up from the back of its shaggy carapace. It ran on eight legs, while keeping its two forelegs—which ended in smallish claws, for a crab—extended in front of it, pincers open, as if ready to grab.

"Jesus," Fuseli said, looking out at it. "It's coming right for us, isn't it?"

He hadn't forgotten it existed; none of them had. However, the crab being hadn't come around again since Tarragon had seen it clamber up the side of the crater named Gertrude, and despite its size it hadn't been spotted again despite a few drone sweeps. They'd given up after that and hadn't devoted much thought to it, in light of other matters they'd had to contend with.

The assumption had been that the creature had gone off to explore elsewhere, most likely to die for lack of nourishment no matter how hardy it was. Given its furry coat and the fact that it appeared adapted for a cold environment, Fuseli had thought it might even have hidden away in some cave to enter into hibernation—or at least to go dormant, as some terrestrial crabs would do for months at a time.

"Doesn't this shuttle have a gun?" Anthony Nguyen cried, leaning across the aisle to watch the approaching creature, too.

"No," Tarragon said with grim flatness.

"*No?* Why the hell is it so far from the base to the launch pads? Didn't these people ever think how vulnerable they are out here, with all their talk about pirate attacks?"

"We should go back," Amaka said, "shouldn't we? We're closer to the base than to the ship!"

Fuseli squeezed through the center aisle to the tram's front cabin, and rang the buzzer. The door slid open, revealing the tram's pilot was a vaguely insect-like robot, which of course was completely unruffled behind its controls. A tech sat beside it, though, and turned in her seat.

"Can this thing go any faster?" Fuseli asked her.

"No, sir," said the tech. "But the tube we're going through is pretty strong."

"I guess we'll see if that's true."

The tech nodded nervously, obviously no more reassured by her own words than he was.

Fuseli leaned down to peer out the cabin's side window, to observe the creature again. It was still scrabbling in that slow, dream-like way in their direction... looking like the disembodied, skeletal hand of a god.

At this point Fuseli could better make out the details of its head. Whereas the Coleopteroids had a beetle-like face, this thing ventured closer to the fish-like or even mammalian in that regard. It clearly possessed fanged jaws instead of a crustacean's mandibles and maxillipeds, and it was without antennae. The nose was a skull-like cavity, and rather than being on the ends of stalks, its eyes were set back in deep bony sockets, and even featured eyelids. And instead of being entirely black, this thing's eyes seemed to have sclera, irises, and pupils. In fact, he realized its irises were crimson.

The crab being was also close enough now that Fuseli could hear a sound it was making, even through the tram and the tube enclosing its track. It was like the sound of an entire beehive stirred to fury...but with that sound both greatly magnified and ominously slowed down in speed. Fuseli began to feel that buzzing as a vibration in his own body.

"It's going to reach us!" the tech cried out.

Fuseli switched his gaze to the front window. Launch Station 3 was in sight. The Khopesh waiting on Launch Pad 3-B. They were about halfway there...

Then, the crab struck.

It had bunched its long, multiply-jointed legs and launched itself off the ground for the rest of the way...sailing almost gracefully through the airlessness, before suddenly crashing down upon the tram tube.

Then, in addition to the crab being's deep, bone-rattling buzzing sound, inside the tram they could also hear a high-pitched squealing as the thing's toothy pincers fought to catch onto the tube's smooth surface, and crush it.

The creature kept up with the tram as it glided along, undaunted by its failure to crush the tube with its pincers. Now, it took to hammering its claws down on top of the curved tube instead, as it continued crawling alongside. Outside, its face loomed close now, and though it was composed of hard plates and lacked the muscles to convey expression, its fearsome mask-like visage still managed to project seething rage.

Fuseli knew this wasn't like some mindless animal simply attracted to movement, like a cat chasing a flashlight's beam. It was a sentient being that saw them as an enemy, and it wanted to kill them. He felt it surely must blame them for it having been stolen here from its own world.

Unless...unless, it was being used by someone else, as a weapon...

He returned to the passenger cabin, his eyes fixed on Yarlath.

"It's going to break through!" Nguyen shouted, eyes wild. "You don't have enough spacesuits in here for all of us if that happens, do you? If this shuttle gets compromised?"

"Unfortunately that's right," Fuseli shouted back, squeezing past to get to Yarlath. They could barely hear each other over the crab being's buzzing. "Morris, do you have a knife on you?"

"I got this." From a pocket of his camos, Tarragon produced the steak knife Rhan had sneaked out of the cafeteria, and which he had confiscated. He handed it to Fuseli, who continued with it on to Yarlath.

Fuseli stood over the Man from the Plane and said, "I'm going to stab you now, Mr. Yarlath. Are you okay with that?"

Yarlath didn't respond, his head still tilted back, his eyes still closed, that composed almost a smile on his lips. The only answer was another boom from the crab being as it slammed one of its claws down on the tube again.

"Hey! Hey—look!" one of the Colonial Forcers cried, as he faced out the rear window, past the freight car containing the drugged Companion.

The others followed his pointing finger, and saw one of the base's transport rovers out there behind them, bouncing along at top speed on its three pairs of wheels. It was going faster than the tram, rushing to catch up.

Fuseli's wrist comp was beeping, alerting him to a call, but he ignored it. He was in the middle of something. He leaned down over Yarlath, cocked back his arm, and then brought the knife down with force. He buried its blade to the handle in the top of Yarlath's right leg.

Again, not even a quiver of Yarlath's face.

"He has to be out for real," Tarragon said. Then, his wrist comp started beeping, too, and he took the call.

Fuseli left the knife in place. He'd remove the blade and patch the wound once they were in the Khopesh. If they *made it* to the Khopesh.

"It's Tamati in the rover!" Tarragon called out. "They spotted the thing coming into the crater on a security drone!"

"Good old Rhys," Fuseli said, looking out the windows again. "If he gets here in time."

"We're almost to the launch station!" Amaka cried.

"Oh, please God!" Rhan said.

Though there was no air outside to provide a medium for sound, there was air inside the tram, and at that moment a tremendous crash reached them—along with a violent shudder. Outside, the crab being had finally slammed one of its claws on the tube's top with sufficient force to break through. The tube was constructed of many linked sections, but that section was shattered, and immediately the crab thrust its foreleg into the tube through the opening and groped after them, snapping its pincers. However, the tram continued onward and eluded its reach, leaving the crab to clutch at them in vain, its entire long forelimb inserted into the tube.

One of the Colonial Forcers pointed his Drang toward the cabin's rear window, eyes crazed with fear, but Amaka grabbed his arm. "Hey, watch it! What are you going to do, shoot through the window and suck all the air out?"

Tarragon heard this and growled to the young C-Forcer, "Keep it together, soldier!"

As they watched the creature remove its arm from the tube and start crawling after them again, trying to regain lost ground, they saw the rover closing the distance between them.

"If that thing makes it to the launch station," Nguyen said, "it can attack the ship itself!"

"There's no way it could get into the ship," Tarragon said. "This tram, maybe, but not that ship."

"But we won't be able to get *into* the ship if it's right outside!"

"Here comes Rhys," Fuseli said.

The rover was coming up on the crab being's right. Until now, the creature either hadn't noticed it was being pursued—perhaps because it couldn't hear any sound from the rover—or else it had been too intent on getting at the tram. Now, though, it slowed its own pursuit and started to wheel around to confront the small ground vehicle, raising both its claws in front of it, ready to lash out...

The rover was equipped with a mounted gun, and from this blazed a stream of blinding white energy bolts that lit up the surrounding ice.

The passengers continued watching out the back of the tram even as it began to pull into the little tram station for Launch Station 3. They saw one of the crab being's forelegs blown off completely and go spinning away, as more energy bolts penetrated the exoskeleton its thick fur was rooted in. The crab being opened wide its mouth, filled with combs of fangs like those of some deep sea fish, as if to howl in frustration and agony, but inside the tram all that reached them was that same deep buzzing tone.

The rover stopped advancing and remained at a safe distance from the crab being, but kept pouring on the firepower.

The crab being tried to remain standing on its eight stilt-like legs—tried to push itself toward the rover as if walking into a hurricane wind—but it had finally sustained too much damage. It collapsed where it stood, holes burned through its chitin armor in dozens of places, its fur singed black in those spots, and one of its two glaring red eyes shot out. The buzzing sound had finally ceased.

"That's one specimen I guess they won't be getting back at Port Haven," Fuseli remarked, as he turned from the windows and went to Rhan, to put a hand on her shoulder.

As the tram slowed to a stop inside the station, Tarragon answered another call on his wrist comp. On the device's screen, Rhys Tamati smiled through the faceplate of his helmet. His blue-glowing face tattoo softly illuminated its interior.

"You folks good, now?" Tamati asked.

"Well done, man," Tarragon told him.

PART SIX:

The Khopesh

-1-

While the pallet onto which the Companion had been lashed down with a whole row of shipping straps was being carried by a forklift robot up a ramp and into the cargo hold behind the E.C.S. Khopesh's passenger cabin, Fuseli patched the wound in Yarlath's leg. Neither the Man from the Plane nor the Companion had yet showed any sign of regaining consciousness. Fuseli had some more syringes on him if they did.

Watching Fuseli clean up after the modest operation, Tarragon said, "What if they have a bad reaction to the drug, and go into a coma or something?"

"Then I'll advocate for euthanizing the poor things." Fuseli stowed away the first aid kit, then moved on to where Rhan was sitting and leaned over her to speak to her quietly. "How are you holding up, lady?"

"Better, with that crab thing dead." She looked both reassured but nervous as the small military patrol ship thrummed with life, pilot Dalia Halabi and copilot Christopher Rix up front powering up the craft and running their last checks before takeoff. "It's not far to this space station, right?"

"Not far at all. It's lower in the atmosphere, to harvest gas, but it's right out there in orbit like this moon...just a hop, skip, and a jump away."

Rhan sighed. "Okay. Can you please sit beside me for the flight?"

Fuseli looked into her eyes for several seconds, hesitating, and then said, "Sure." She scooted over into the seat closer to the bulkhead, while Fuseli took the seat she had occupied. "When we get there," he reassured her, "we'll get you settled fast and hopefully you can get some proper sleep. And that guy over there...we'll keep him drugged, and stow him on the other side of the station just like we did here."

"It seems like no place is really far enough away to be safe," she said. "You remember what I told you, about how Yarlath's people are really just puppets for those Dweller things? If the one that controls him still has power over him this far away...in a whole other dimension..."

Fuseli just stared at her gravely. What could he say to that? They knew so little about the true extent of Yarlath's abilities, apparently granted to him by that extradimensional iteration of himself.

Then Halabi's voice came over a speaker from the cockpit. "Is everyone set back there for liftoff?"

Fuseli glanced around at his fellow passengers: Amaka Sunday and the other three C-Forcers belted into their seats, Tarragon in the last row sitting across the aisle from the mannequin-silent Yarlath, and Anthony Nguyen resting his head back against his seat and shutting his eyes. In doing so, he looked eerily similar to how Yarlath looked right now.

Fuseli spoke up, knowing the pilots were listening for his reply. "We're ready to roll," he told them.

"Oh my God!" cried Antony Nguyen, gaping straight up at the sky.

There, a vortex composed of red-glowing, half-amorphous bodies spiraled like a living galaxy. So tightly grouped were these bizarre entities that they almost formed a single vast body.

"Actually, they are rather like our gods, aren't they?" said a voice behind him, and he spun toward it.

Together, he and Yarlath stood upon an immeasurable plain of black metal—

inset with strange geometric patterns, throbbing with red light—that gave the impression of stretching off into infinity in all directions, rather than curving like the surface of a planet. In one direction, though, a misty city of black metal reared against the sky of greenish-black storm clouds, this cityscape dominated by a monstrous black pyramid.

Yarlath's nose no longer appeared broken, black blood no longer staining the front of his top, nor his leg where Fuseli had planted a knife in him. He said, "Though, if that is the case, then aren't we the gods, ourselves? You see how every universe—all creation, all that exists—is so wondrously linked? Every individual in your reality has a counterpart like me. A counterpart like *them.*" He jerked his head up toward the vortex. "You were going to ask me where you are. This is the Plane. This is their domain." This time he pointed above him. "But they brought my kind here, because by extension their home is our home. Well, it was...until those savages ripped me from it. They're like children playing with fire, aren't they? It's a miracle you weren't killed as a result of their blind fumbling."

"Am I really here?" Nguyen stammered, looking up at that hurricane of tentacled bodies.

"Unfortunately, no. This is simply my way of sharing it with you. This is the mode in which we can speak privately, you and I."

"It's Hell!" Nguyen blurted. "And you're a demon!"

"Don't be foolish, Anthony. I'm not your enemy...*they* are. The ones who imprisoned you, and imprisoned me, too. Don't you see that? And what did they promise you for assisting them in their research? Total freedom, wasn't it?"

"No," Nguyen said. "They halved my sentence...from twenty years to ten."

Yarlath winced. "Ten years. That's a long time for your kind, isn't it? You risked your life for them for *that?*"

"Please...let me go back! I don't want to be here!"

"Calm down, Anthony. You're in that ship of theirs, the same as me. You're peacefully resting there right now. *Just like me.*"

"What do you want from me?"

Yarlath sighed, and he himself gazed up at the thousands of seething bodies in their whirlpool-like formation. "I can't allow myself to become trapped in their realm for the rest of my existence. Just a prisoner, like you. Humiliated... disrespected by my inferiors. I would prefer death to that, Anthony."

"Then just kill yourself, why don't you?"

"Well...I did try," he admitted. "When I had my rather primitive iteration outside attack that little shuttle of theirs. I had no illusions about surviving, if it managed to break into it and compromise its air. I hoped at least to take my enemies with me. However, I suppose I can't be too sorry that my attempt failed, because now I see another possibility...one in which perhaps I don't need to die, after all. And *that*, Anthony, is where you come in."

"How? You tried to kill me and all the others along with you, and now you want me to help you?"

"Anthony, when will you realize...we are the same self. We are more than brothers, more close than parent and child! Your loyalty should be to *me!*"

"I didn't say I was loyal to them."

"I offer you full freedom...not half freedom."

"So how, then?"

"You belonged to some criminal band, did you not? I've heard them discussing such things, while they took me to be unconscious."

"You're not unconscious?"

"My body has been immobilized by their drug, but my mind remains fully active. Well, to be fair, I do feel somewhat impaired. I had difficulty directing that creature to attack the shuttle, and now I'm struggling to direct my Companion..."

"What were you saying about my gang?" Nguyen demanded.

"They pilot their own spacecraft and raid other vessels, things of that nature, do they not?"

"Yes. They call us pirates."

"And do you know how to fly a spacecraft yourself, Anthony?"

"Yes. Small ships."

"Small? Like, for instance, the one you and I are prisoners in right now?"

"What are you proposing? Just tell me!"

Yarlath said, "I propose, Anthony, that working together, we take control of this ship...and then, you can pilot it to the closet outpost of that gang of yours."

"Are you kidding?" Nguyen cried. "Do you see what you're up against in that ship? Except for you, me, and Rhan they're all Colonial Forcers! Fuseli and Tarragon are Special Ops! We wouldn't stand a chance!"

"You might be right," Yarlath said calmly. One might say, fatalistically. "In fact, you probably are. But what other chance do we have? There will be even more of them to oppose us if we make it to this Port Urano where we'll soon be arriving. As I told you, Anthony—I would rather die than become their prisoner for life. And what about you? Don't you have any pride? Are you willing to let these monsters continue to humiliate *you?* Disrespect *you?*"

"Oh no...no." Nguyen began backing away from Yarlath, even though there was nowhere to back away *to*. Not here, in his own mind. "I'd rather spend ten years in prison than throw the rest of my life away!"

"Now you're sounding pathetic, Anthony. You're making me quite disappointed in you."

"Be disappointed all you want!" Nguyen shouted, veins standing out in his neck. "I won't give you my life!"

"Then I'm afraid I'll simply have to take it from you, Anthony," Yarlath said. "I was hoping you'd make this easier, since I need you to pilot that ship for me... but we'll make do. We'll make do..."

-2-

Being a military craft and designed to take enemy fire, the Khopesh's passenger cabin had no windows, but Rhan watched the screen inset into the back of the seat in front of her as the patrol ship left Titania far below. And then, out here in space, there was no above or below...just distances between here and there.

She reached over to Fuseli with one hand and linked her fingers through his. He rubbed his thumb over the top of her hand soothingly. With his free hand, Fuseli adjusted the screen's view to show her a patrol craft identical to the Khopesh, moving toward the blue crescent of Uranus ahead of them. He zoomed in on it a bit. "That's the Assegai," he told her.

"The hearse," she said.

"Huh. I guess it kind of is."

Rhan grunted, then slid down into her seat a little, trying to get comfortable. "You can turn it off now," she told him, closing her eyes. "It's giving me vertigo."

Meanwhile in the row behind them, on the opposite side of the aisle, Anthony Nguyen opened his eyes and lifted his head from his seat rest. "I need to use the toilet," he announced to the man seated beside him, a soldier named Private Rusk. Rusk was the young Colonial Forcer whom Tarragon had chided for almost panicking and firing at the crab being through the tram's rear window.

Rusk asked him, "What do you need to do?"

"I need to move my bowels."

Rusk snorted and mimicked him. "You need to 'move your bowels'? You can hold it until we get there."

"Can I please at least empty my bladder?" Nguyen persisted.

Tarragon was listening in from the row behind them. "Let him go. The john is right at the back, Nguyen."

"Thank you." He stood from his seat and Rusk got up to let him squeeze out into the aisle. "Can I have my hands freed?"

"You can handle your pecker just fine with your hands cuffed, pirate," Rusk told him, sitting back down in his seat.

Nguyen sighed and moved toward the back of the passenger cabin. The main access to the cargo hold was at the rear of the ship, but it could also be accessed from here within the passenger's cabin, through a sealed door at its very end. Just to the left of this door was the craft's single, closet-like toilet.

Nguyen came to a stop at the rear wall, and with his back to the others it was not apparent at first what he was doing. However, it only took Tarragon a second to become suspicious, and just as he was twisting around in his seat to ask Nguyen if he was lost, Nguyen had reached out with his cuffed hands and punched the button to open the cargo hold's inner door. Even as it slid back—and Tarragon started up from his seat—Nguyen ducked sideways through the open door of the little toilet, shielding himself from what burst free from the cargo hold. From the thing that had been waiting silently on the other side...

The Companion looked as though it had been mercilessly tortured while inside the cargo hold, but the injuries it bore had been self inflicted. Across its torso and heavy thighs the crimson-skinned proto-human bore long, deep lacerations, from having exerted pressure against the shipping bands that had strapped it down on its pallet. It had burst these straps, without concern for the pain the effort brought. But more shocking than this, to escape the manacles that had bound both its wrists and ankles, the Companion had used its powerful jaws and pronounced incisors to tear through its own limbs, as a coyote might chew through its leg to escape from a trap.

Yarlath had tried to direct the Companion to chew through only one wrist, which would allow the manacles to dangle off the remaining, intact hand...and to chew through only one ankle, thereby dragging the manacles from the remaining foot. However, the Companion had become too frenzied, too filled with bloodlust for its master's enemies, and had misinterpreted the command. Therefore, the grotesquely mangled creature that lunged into the Khopesh's passenger cabin from the cargo hold ran on all fours like a gorilla, and all four limbs ended in a ragged, bleeding stump.

In the row nearest to the back, across the aisle from the blissful-looking Yarlath, Tarragon had bolted up from his seat and was reaching to the ceiling. The Colonial Forcers onboard had stowed their Drang assault engines in an overhead rack that ran the length of the passenger cabin for easy access, since the ship's usual passengers were military personnel. Before he could detach the gun, however, the Companion swung one of its powerfully muscled arms. The impact sent Tarragon crashing back, sprawling across several seats with his head slamming into the wall.

In the next row beyond, Private Ruck had gone for his own Drang, and he managed to pull it free just as the Companion reached him. Without hands, it couldn't grasp him, so instead it wrapped one arm around his body and drew the young C-Forcer against its chest. Pinned there, thrashing helplessly, Ruck looked up into the Companion's furious face. Its chin was already slathered with its own blood, bits of its own flesh jammed between its teeth, and this was what Ruck saw as the Companion clamped its jaws onto his screaming face.

As the Companion shook its head viciously from side to side, separating Ruck's flesh from the bone beneath, Ruck blindly triggered his assault engine. An automatic stream of projectiles flashed from one of the bulky gun's three muzzles.

Ahead of the Companion and its prey, the other three Colonial Forcers had shot up from their seats and were also detaching their Drangs from the overhead rack. Private Amaka Sunday got her gun down and activated first, but either purposely or accidentally, the Companion had Ruck's body in front of it like a shield. Amaka began to shoulder her weapon to aim more carefully through its targeting screen, intending to focus on the proto-human's head, but that was when Ruck's own gun released its wild spray of bullets.

As soon as the Companion had entered the cabin, Fuseli had shoved Rhan down in her seat and pulled his Scythe handgun. He had no Drang of his own within arm's reach. He swung out of his seat into the aisle, but kept low, trying to see around the risen Colonial Forcers to assess the situation...and hoping for a clear shot at the Companion, himself.

Ruck's spasm of gunfire strafed across the two Colonial Forcers closest to him. One of them was Amaka Sunday, who was for the second time during this assignment struck across the chest armor. Only one of the projectiles pierced her, in the upper left arm, but it tore through messily. She went down with a cry, her arm hanging half off.

The burly C-Forcer beside her, despite wearing his body armor and helmet for this flight as the other soldiers did, took two projectiles through the neck. His spinal column severed, he was dead before he even crumpled to the floor of the aisle with Amaka.

Rusk's face came away from its skull, and the Companion let his limp body fall. Even as it did so, the proto-human surged forward toward the last standing Colonial Forcer, a stony-faced young woman, who with Rusk out of the way opened up with her Drang. From the floor, supporting her Drang with her one good arm, Amaka fired at the oncoming Companion, too. And behind them, Fuseli opened up with his Scythe.

Somehow, even in the face of this onslaught, the Companion came barreling at them on the stumps of its four limbs, which left a spoor of blood splats in its wake. The bullets they put into the creature blasted gaping exit wounds across its back. It seemed the Companion would bowl them all over...even continue on into the cockpit itself...

In terror, no longer so stony-faced, the last standing C-Forcer jumped back to get out of the Companion's way, but too late. It slammed into her legs, knocking her to the floor and lying half on top of her, pinning her down. It was only then that she, and Fuseli both, realized the thing was dead.

Fuseli looked across the scene of carnage, gauging the losses. Being a combat surgeon, his mindset was triage. Amaka was alive, Rusk and the burly C-Forcer dead. From back here he only saw Tarragon's legs protruding into the aisle, so he couldn't be sure about his friend. Behind him, he knew Rhan was unhurt.

He bent down to help the C-Forcer pinned by the Companion get out from under its bullet-riddled bulk.

"Holy fuck," the young woman panted, exhilarated to still be alive, "I thought it had me, too!"

Fuseli was in no mood to be exhilarated...not until he found out Tarragon's condition. As soon as he had roughly hoisted the C-Forcer to her feet, he ordered her, "Grab the first aid and get an emergency patch on Private Sunday's arm!"

Then, he turned toward the rear of the cabin, thinking that the Companion had let itself in through the cargo hold door. He hadn't seen Nguyen back there before...but he saw him now.

Nguyen smiled at him, holding a Scythe handgun in front of him in both hands to steady its aim, despite his wrists still being shackled. He had emerged from the toilet he'd ducked into, and taken the pistol from the belt holster of the downed Morris Tarragon.

"Hello, Dr. Fuseli," Nguyen said, and then he fired one shot.

The bullet struck Fuseli under the left collar bone. He wasn't wearing chest armor as the Colonial Forces grunts did, and the shot spun him down to the floor.

The stony-faced C-Forcer had crouched down beside Amaka, having grabbed a first aid kit as directed, and she whipped her head around in time to see Nguyen switch his aim to her. He shot her once in the face, and she dropped across Amaka, who lay there losing blood and going into shock.

"Well, well, well," Nguyen said, looking around him at the heaped bodies, "this actually went better than I expected." He turned to look down at the unconscious figure of Yarlath. That is, to look down at his own body. "Now...if only I'd wake up." He leaned in closer to examine his own placid face. "I certainly hope I can! I'd hate to remain in this second-rate vessel."

"Hey," said a voice behind him.

Nguyen wasn't as uncannily fast as Yarlath, despite Yarlath presently using him as a vehicle. He turned around quickly, but not quickly enough. He did see, though—just before she opened fire—Rhan Luyen aiming a pistol, held in both hands to keep it steady just as he had done. It was Fuseli's Scythe, which she had snatched out of his hand.

"Wait!" Nguyen began to say, starting to bring his own gun up...but too late...

Rhan fired. Once, and then twice for good measure.

Nguyen flinched, and actually looked down at his body, expecting to see holes in his chest. He had felt no impacts. He lowered his own handgun and spun around to look behind him in sudden understanding.

Yarlath still wore that peaceful little smile, even with the top of his bald head shot off down to the eyebrows. Black blood poured forth copiously as if overflowing from a volcano's crater, soon covering the paper-white skin of his face.

"Take it easy, sister!" Nguyen said, tossing away from him the gun he'd been holding. He then held his cuffed arms above his head. "Whatever I did, I didn't do it!"

"I know that," Rhan told him. "That's why I didn't shoot you."

Fuseli had forced himself to his feet beside her, and she allowed him to gently take the gun from her hands. "Rhan...go see if Lieutenant Tarragon is alive," he groaned.

"Sit down, Robert!" She eased him into his seat.

Nguyen had moved to where Tarragon was sprawled across two seats, bending over him. "He's still breathing!" he called.

Fuseli winced with pain, and said, "Okay then, Rhan, can you get a dressing on Private Sunday's arm before she bleeds out?"

"I got it!" a new voice cried. Fuseli looked over to see that the copilot, Christopher Rix, had emerged from the cockpit. He hurried to squat down beside

Amaka, who looked up at him dazedly, barely clinging to consciousness. "What happened back here, Captain? Is it all over?"

"It's over," Fuseli said, looking into Rhan's concerned face as she pressed a palm against the entrance wound in his upper chest. "Yarlath and his pet are dead. Just as I would have preferred them to be in the first place."

As Rix tore into the first aid kit to see to Amaka, he said, "We're almost there, Captain. Just hold on, and I'll put a patch on you next."

"I'd very much appreciate that, Lieutenant."

Rhan whispered to Fuseli, "I guess he forgot I'm a murderer, too."

Nguyen stepped over dead bodies to come closer to them. "Look, Captain...it wasn't me. You know that, right? They won't blame me for any of this, will they? I tried to resist him...I did!"

"I believe you, Tony Nguyen," Fuseli mumbled, as he began to lose consciousness, himself.

Now he had two murderers he was determined to protect. Or, in a way, two versions of one.

PART SEVEN:

Port Urano

"Stabbed. Shot," said General Aaron Stroud. "You're getting old, Bob."

"Hey, Morris is getting slow, too," Fuseli said, propped in a bed in Port Urano's med unit and looking into his wrist comp. "It isn't just me."

"Thanks," Tarragon said, sitting in a chair nearby. He'd had two ribs broken, besides his concussion.

Fuseli had a nasty exit wound in his back and a shattered scapula that would be more properly tended to once they were transported from Port Urano to Port Haven by the military destroyer that was on the way, but for now his collapsed lung had been sealed so it could reinflate.

"Terrible waste of life, over there," Stroud said. "As if all the people they lost in that explosion wasn't enough."

"I should have drugged Nguyen, too," Fuseli said, his manner becoming more grave. "Even Rhan, so he couldn't have made use of either of them."

"Hey, don't go blaming yourself. Yarlath's body never came out from the drug's effect, you told me...right up to the end. Right? How could you know his mind was still aware?"

"If I'd had my way, he and his Companion would have been bagged in the Assegai's cargo hold before we even left Gertrude."

"Well, I'd have to share that sentiment, but we had our orders, Bob. We had our orders."

When Stroud had signed off, Fuseli turned toward Private Amaka Sunday, who lay in another hospital-style bed a short distance away. "You might not know this," Fuseli told her, "but General Stroud has two prosthetic legs, and he gets around on them just fine."

"I know," said Amaka, whose severely damaged arm had needed to be amputated. "I hear he lost them in the Red War."

"Maybe you could get yourself one of the same type of prosthetic arms the Coleopteroids use," he told her. "You know, they remove their perfectly healthy limbs on purpose just so they can use those instead."

"Oh, that would be *lovely*, Captain," Amaka said. "You can be sure I'll request one just like that."

Not even one Earth day since they'd arrived at Port Urano, Fuseli and Rhan Luyen—who sat in a chair pulled close to his hospital bed—watched a screen mounted on the opposite wall, as the great destroyer dispatched from Port Haven came smoothly in to dock. Its medical team would be coming immediately to move the injured aboard. Used to fighting conflicts in far, harsh locations, their crew were better equipped for emergencies than those here at this orbital helium-3 mining station, and would see to it that Fuseli, Amaka, Tarragon, Base Gertrude maintenance tech Oskar Karlsson, and the two other injured Colonial Forces soldiers reached Port Haven as comfortably as possible.

Rhan held his hand under the light blanket that covered him, and with her back shielding her actions from Amaka in the next bed, shy about the young Colonial Forcer seeing that she did so.

She asked Fuseli, "Robert...do you think Dr. Marceau and those others will succeed with their teleportation experiments?"

"With the Coleopteroids only helping next time, and not sabotaging, I think they will in the near future."

"And even though the Coleopteroids haven't ever found my world before, do you think it's possible that either your people or their people *will* be able to go there, someday?"

This wasn't the first time she'd asked him this, but now he was inclined to answer more tenderly. "It's possible, Rhan. If you could come here accidentally, you might one day be able to go back on purpose. I don't want to discourage you, but I don't want to get your hopes up, either. As we've both seen, there are a hell of a lot of other universes out there. Or should I say, right here, all around us... laid over this one."

"I know I've said my daughter is better off never seeing me again, but I don't want her to remember me only as a killer, Robert." She looked from the wall screen to his face. "And I don't want you to think of me only as a killer, either."

He squeezed her hand under the blanket.

"Nor do I want you to only see *me* that way," he told her. "But hey...we killers do have to stick together."

ABOUT THE AUTHOR

Jeffrey Thomas is the author of the dark science fiction series Punktown, which was introduced with the collection *Punktown* (Ministry of Whimsy Press, 2000) and includes the novels *Monstrocity* (Prime Books, 2003; Bram Stoker Award finalist), *Deadstock* (Solaris Books, 2007; John W. Campbell Award finalist), and *Blue War* (Solaris Books, 2008). His other books include the short story collection *The Unnamed Country* (Word Horde, 2019), the novel *The American* (JournalStone, 2020), and the Hades Trilogy (Weird House Press, 2023). His stories have been reprinted in *The Year's Best Horror Stories* XXII (editor, Karl Edward Wagner), *The Year's Best Fantasy and Horror* #14 (editors, Ellen Datlow and Terri Windling), and *Year's Best Weird Fiction* #1 (editors, Laird Barron and Michael Kelly). Thomas lives in Massachusetts.

ABOUT THE ARTIST

Frank Walls is an American artist best known for his dark, surrealistic fine art, fantasy illustration, and similarly ominous heavy metal musicianship.

Walls' interests in heavy metal music, dark art, and horror films paved the way to his emergence as the lead vocalist for bands like Embalmer and HateWorks in the mid to late 90's. His passion for fine art underlined his guttural vocals, and he produced CD and t-shirt art for bands like Incantation and Crypt Kicker, while front lining others. This era of artistic experimentation paved the way for his immersion in The Cleveland Institute of Art, where he focused on illustration and graduated with a BFA.

As a post-graduate Walls designed and illustrated book covers for authors such as Jeffrey Thomas, Shane Mckenzie, and Jeff Strand, while pursuing illustration work in the fantasy realm - what would become the backbone of his career. Walls is celebrated for his contributions to game companies like Fantasy Flight Games, Wizards of the Coast, and Alderac Entertainment. In 2015 Walls co-founded his own company Noctis Games.

Walls now hails from Hawaii where he teaches Art and Design, works as a freelance illustrator, and pursues his passion for painting.

WEIRD
HOUSE

www.ingramcontent.com/pod-product-compliance
Lightning Source LLC
LaVergne TN
LVHW090946080826
845145LV00003B/905

* 9 7 8 1 9 5 7 1 2 1 7 3 4 *